THAT WOMAN ON THISTLEDOWN LANE

D. E. MALONE

That Woman on Thistledown Lane
Copyright © 2023 D.E. Malone
All rights reserved.
Cover designed by Red Leaf Book Design
Library of Congress Cataloging-in-Publication Data has been applied for

For exclusive content and book news, subscribe to D.E. Malone's *Welcome to the Sweet Life* newsletter.

Chapter One

Weeds, like certain memories, had the habit of popping up with relentless annoyance.

The more Janie Wendell snipped and pulled, the more the pesky honeysuckle shoots poked through the spongey soil in her parents' lush yard. And the moist earth soaked through her gardening gloves in a hurry, rendering them useless in keeping Janie's hands dry and warm.

She straightened to relieve the kink in her back and surveyed her progress with the clippers on this particular flower bed. With the relentless rain last month, the normally immaculate landscaping around Aaron and Sonya Wendell's property had taken on a life of its own. The wild honeysuckle was particularly troublesome.

Janie twisted at the waist, feeling her muscles sigh with relief. This was a far cry from working the tables at Daisy Gap Cafe, that was for sure. Janie was using muscles she forgot she had.

"Maybe that's enough work for this morning," her mother mused from the lawn chair a few feet away. Sonya Wendell had been keeping Janie company as her daughter moved from flower bed to flower bed around the verdant property.

"Nonsense." Janie dropped the pruners and stripped off the gloves, laying them over the back of her own chair before moving it into a sunny spot to hasten the drying time. "Despite the aches, I'm feeling pretty good. The foliage doesn't make bothersome demands like the cafe customers."

Sonya chuckled. "But unlike your paying customers, the foliage is pretty cheap in the tipping department."

"Honestly, sometimes I'd rather keep company with weeds than some people."

"I understand that more than you know." Sonya shifted in her chair, causing it to creak.

Beyond the circular flower bed, her sister Rose's twins jumped into the sandbox next to the deck, whooping with delight. Rose sat in a lounge chair next to the sandbox, talking with Janie's father while they sipped lemonade.

Janie caught Sonya's wince from the corner of her eye as her mother moved her leg where it was propped on another chair.

"Can I get you something?" Janie glanced at her watch. Her mother was almost due for another dose of the pain medication that was never too far away. Janie eyed the wrap around Sonya's lower leg and the thin tube of a PICC line taped to her arm. The familiar queasiness rippled through Janie too before she had a chance to avert her eyes. She hated that thing, how it was tangible proof of her mother's vulnerability.

Sonya gritted her teeth. "No, I'm going to push through a little longer. I hate relying on that stuff."

Janie leaned forward to help her mother reposition the thin cushion underneath her calf. It was little things like this that reminded Janie she was needed here in Port Chance. Already a few weeks had passed since coming home, and Janie was beginning to feel settled again. It helped that she'd finally unpacked the last stack of boxes and found a place for everything. The quaint garden guest house at the back of her parents' property was smaller than her two-bedroom bungalow in Hendricks, Minnesota, but she'd miraculously managed to fit everything she owned inside.

"But remember what your doctor said about staying on top of the pain. It's harder to get it under control again if it gets too bad."

Sonya grumbled. She leaned her head against the chair back and closed her eyes.

Almost sixty, Sonya Wendell possessed a natural beauty. Her fair skin had pinkened as the mid-morning sun crept from behind the overgrown lilac bushes. Wisps of her amber hair floated around her face. Her mother had never colored her hair, choosing to let it be overtaken naturally by softer shades of gray. Janie inherited her mother's coloring and her father's dark eyes.

"I've never been a slave to pain, and I'm not going to start now," Sonya said, her eyes still closed.

"You've also never had to deal with something this potentially serious."

Sonya frowned but was silent. A cue for Janie to leave the topic be.

Janie eyed Sonya's leg wrap again and felt gooseflesh populate the skin along her arms. The angry, red welt underneath the bandage was worse than she expected when she first saw the injury. It hadn't started out like that, her father had said. Shortly after she'd scraped her shin on a broken branch in knee-high flood water, Sonya was in the hospital getting the PICC line to fight an infection. It'd been a battle since then to keep the infection at bay let alone knock it out.

Janie took a sip of lemonade and picked up her phone. Another unknown call came through again while she'd been weeding. Same number. No voice message. That made four since last week. She never answered unknown numbers, choosing instead to let them go straight to voicemail if they left messages. Then she blocked the spam calls. Janie quickly scrolled through her emails, closed her inbox, and set the phone back in the drink holder of her chair.

"I should head inside to get cleaned up. Monte wants to go over some new menu items." She eyed the four-by-four post she'd sunk into concrete two days ago. "I might try to attach the birdhouse tomorrow. The cement should be set."

"That would be perfect. The little wrens have been yelling at me. The two houses that were knocked down by the storms are always filled with babies this time of year."

"I think they were scolding me too for being slow yesterday." She liked working with her hands. Building the new birdhouses to replace the damaged ones was a small but satisfying project. Using her father's power tools, it'd taken her less time than it took to cover the lunch rush at the diner.

Sonya sighed and smiled. "I bet he loves having you back. I swear there's been a 'help wanted' sign in his window since you left."

"That's because his fiancée chases away the waitresses because she thinks everyone is out to steal her Monte away." Janie stood again and picked up the clippers. Another honeysuckle shoot in the midst of the lilac bush caught her eye. She snipped it as close to the ground as she could manage.

Her old boss and owner of the Daisy Gap Cafe, Monte

Freed, managed to get engaged while Janie was away. His fiancée, Camilla, kept one eye on the oven and one eye on Janie over the last two weeks whenever she got too close to Monte. The fact that Janie had never harbored any romantic feelings for Monte didn't seem to register with Camilla. Janie wondered how long short-tempered Monte would tolerate his soon-to-be wife treating the staff like they were all romantic rivals.

"And you've somehow won her over?"

Janie nodded. "Easy. I volunteered to watch her son on Saturday night while she and Monte go out."

"You're as wily as they come," Sonya said.

"I'm not above a little gentle coercion. The quicker she learns I'm the least of her worries, the sooner we can all settle into our respective roles." Truthfully, it would have been so much easier to get a waitress job somewhere else. But limiting herself to working in Port Chance, that gave her two options: Daisy Gap Cafe and the Yellow Pier. And considering the Mississippi River carved a temporary channel right through the Yellow Pier last month, Monte's business was her only choice.

Janie turned around again when Sonya's chair creaked underneath her weight. "Do you need help getting back to the house?"

Sonya had lifted her foot from the chair. Her crutches lay in the grass beside her. Janie handed her one, then the other.

"Your dad can help," Sonya said apologetically.

"That's what I'm here for. I only wish I would have come home sooner."

Sonya tucked the crutches underneath her arms. "It wouldn't have changed much. We would have still have had the flood. And you couldn't have prevented this," Sonya said, kicking her bandaged leg out for emphasis.

Janie sighed. It might have been different. Instead of staying away for as long as possible, she could have been here supporting her mother and the rest of the family.

Her mother's expression softened. "You've never been one to look back. To have regrets." She tapped Janie on her leg with the end of a crutch. "Don't change now," she said with a small smile.

"I know. It's that Wendell laser focus." She motioned with both hands straight ahead.

Sonya chuckled. "Your father has referred to it as a curse."

Her mother was on her feet now, almost at eye level with Janie. She reached up to pick something out of Janie's hair—a honeysuckle blossom. The things were everywhere.

"But you're here now, Janie. That's what is important, right?"

Janie wrapped an arm around Sonya's shoulders. Underneath the lightweight cardigan, Sonya's shoulder blades cut into Janie's bicep, and she loosened her grip on her mother. Sonya was a strong, sturdy woman before the infection started robbing her of strength and appetite. It had happened all so quickly. Her fragility reminded Janie her mother wasn't the invincible, larger-than-life presence she'd always known. A flash of annoyance coursed through her, and that irritated Janie even more. As if Sonya had purposely injured herself and invited the bacteria into her body to spite her family.

While she was busy running away from Port Chance, life continued on without her. And now here she was again, the butt of some cosmic joke. The roots of her hometown latched onto her ankles and held on tight like a vine.

Janie had forced herself to settle into the guest house on the back of the property before she begged Monte for her old waitress job at Daisy Gap Cafe. The instant Janie had strolled into the restaurant, at the tail end of the morning rush, Monte spotted her and crowed, "I knew you couldn't stay away!" She'd waited until she was back in the kitchen, where her old boss and his fiancée kept the kitchen running like a well-oiled engine, to ask him about coming back.

And it's been three years, Monte, she reminded him. *It's not like I left yesterday.*

But you're family. It's felt much longer than three years, he'd argued.

Despite the warm welcome, she felt like a failure. A thirty-seven-year-old failure.

Across the lawn, Janie's father spotted Sonya hobbling toward him. He met her halfway to escort her the rest of the way across the patio and into the house.

But then Janie remembered her mother and the trials suffered by so many in her hometown over the last month and a half, and she pushed the poor-me thoughts aside.

Chapter Two

"**T**en!"

Monte bellowed the table number from the small window between the front counter and the kitchen. The busier the diner, the louder he called. What Janie's boss lacked in the height department was made up for in the volume of his lungs. Monte could rattle the rack of water glasses if he had a mind to.

The restaurant hummed with early-afternoon activity. The regulars, mostly white-haired men in flannel shirts and worn leather boots, took up the circular tables in the center of the restaurant. They were a jovial bunch as long as Janie and the other waitress kept their coffees topped off. Janie finished filling the last of their mugs, then headed to pick up the next order.

Monte eyed her through the window when she scooped up the two skillet orders.

"All of Port Chance seems to have come through today, eh?" he said.

She bugged her eyes out. "I was going to ask if I missed

something. Guess everyone is taking a vacation day today. No one's eating at home."

Monte grunted even though the full diner pleased him. Behind Monte, Camilla kept a watchful eye on Janie.

After delivering the food and wiping down three tables, Janie rolled two dozen napkin and utensil sets since the supply from the morning was gone. It wasn't long before another spurt of diners showed up, looking for a respite after shopping on Main Street. While she seated three women who informed her that they'd come for pie and coffee, Monte motioned her back to the window.

"Why don't you take your break during the lull," he said.

She glanced over her shoulder, wondering if Monte was looking at the same dining room she'd been bustling through the last two hours.

"But I have customers with open tabs."

"They can wait," he said brusquely. "Or Billie can close them out. We'll probably be this busy until close. No sense in waiting any longer."

"Then I can—"

Monte shook his head forcefully. "No good. Go now."

Janie untied her apron and balled it up as she breezed past him through the kitchen and out the back door. If Monte saw the stink eye she lobbed his way, he didn't acknowledge it.

Outside, she sank onto her usual spot—the low, brick wall surrounding a raised bed of Monte's herbs, hot peppers, and tomatoes. She picked a few random weeds out of habit, all the while fuming about Monte's treatment. Getting engaged sure hadn't done him any favors; he was as grumpy as ever.

Janie sighed and looked down the alley. A sliver of the Mississippi River flashed between the trees across Water Street.

The sudden urge to escape work and wander along the bank down by Larkspur Park pulled at the part of her that was spontaneous and a little irresponsible. She let out a bitter laugh under her breath. Her carefree days were long over. She wouldn't have entertained the idea of returning to her hometown otherwise.

Her thoughts wandered to her time in Hendricks, the little town in Minnesota that she'd called home for the last three years. Maybe she took the river for granted, having lived alongside it for most of her life, but her reverence for the Big Lake had been much greater. So many times its many moods had matched her own. Calm, unsettled, and playful. Turbulent. She felt a kinship with it. Leaving it behind had wrapped her heartstrings into knots.

The back door creaked open.

"Need you back inside," Monte said.

"You just insisted I—"

"Now."

Unbelievable.

An "I told you so" almost flew out, but Monte had already disappeared.

She glanced again at the sliver of water beckoning her a few blocks away. How quickly a peaceful view and a little quiet time might set her mind at ease. Instead, she flapped her apron a few times to rid it of wrinkles before she tied it around her waist again. Monte might need a talk before the week was over.

Inside, she went straight to Monte's side. He flipped six pancakes onto two plates, garnished each one with a handful of sliced strawberries, and loaded a dollop of whipped cream on top to finish them off.

"Table thirteen needs an order taken," he said flatly as he put the two plates onto the window counter and tapped the bell for Billie to come for them.

The mention of "table thirteen" still gave her a pang of regret. If Monte was the slightest bit observant, he'd give her a little grace and have Billie take over that side of the restaurant until Janie found her footing here again. But no. Table thirteen had no effect on Monte, even though he'd been good friends with the man who'd claimed that table every Friday for months. Years, really. The same man who broke Janie's heart.

"Are you taking their order by teleparty"—Monte whirled one hand around his head—"or are you going to do it the old-fashioned way." Next to him, a little smile quirked Camilla's lips, though she kept her attention on dicing onions.

"I believe you mean 'telepathy' and yes, of course I'm going to get their order."

He lifted his shoulders and shot her a look as if to say, *what's taking so long?*

"We need to talk, Monte." She shifted her weight onto the other foot.

"Oh, you bet we do, darlin'."

If Janie wasn't feeling so abused, she would have doubled over with laughter at Monte's cross look morphing into one of alarm when he realized he'd called her "darling" within earshot of Camilla. He turned his back to Camilla and nodded at the new order pad and a pen on the other side of the griddle.

"Please. It's busier than I thought," he whispered. Was there a smidge of remorse in his tone?

She crossed the dining room, scribbling her name and "13"

on the pad. Out of habit, she almost drew a heart around it, and Janie cringed.

The hum of voices rose and fell in the busy cafe. Another group came through the doors, setting the bells tinkling.

Janie stopped in front of table thirteen while she acknowledged someone who needed attention at another table. *Be right there* she mouthed.

"Hey there, how is your day going so f—"

The next word caught in her throat as the man who'd been studying the menu with his head down looked up. The weight of his surprise threw him back against his seat. *"Janie,"* he breathed.

She blinked, not quite believing he was here, thinking maybe Mark Christie lived in her subconscious so much her mind was playing dirty tricks on her today. Thankfully she had the side of the booth to lean on, or else her knees would have buckled.

"I had...no...idea. It's...you are ..." he sputtered until his voice trailed off.

While her insides curled, she mustered the energy to square her shoulders. "Hi, Mark. What can I get you today?"

He stared for an unbearably long time—long enough for her to almost fall into the hypnotic depths of those sea-green eyes. *Darn that Monte!* He had to be in on this.

Mark visibly shook his head for a reset. "I'm sorry. I didn't expect to see you here today."

"Surprise." Her heart thumped against the wall of her chest like a drum.

"I'll say," he said quietly, looking down at his menu again. He spread his hands palms down on the tabletop, seeming to steady himself before he looked up again. "When did you...get back?"

"Last month."

Her tone was curt, but she couldn't help herself. She grew dizzy and realized she held her breath while her heart skipped erratically. The feeling was so acute she almost pressed her hand against her chest to keep it in check. It was a shock seeing him in front of her, to say the least, and the sour notes of their breakup put a bad taste in her mouth again.

"I'm sure Monte is...happy."

She almost snorted. *Monte, happy*? "I guess."

Mark's chest rose with a deep breath. He laughed humorlessly while he glanced past her toward the kitchen and narrowed his eyes. Yeah, Monte fooled him too, by the looks of it. *Now he'd get creamed from both of us.*

"So, what can I get you?"

He pointed at her and that lopsided smile that had always made her heart flip like one of Monte's hotcakes, spread across his features.

"You..."

"Excuse me?" she croaked. What nerve he had.

"You have—" He pointed to his head, then back to her.

"What?" Janie brushed a hand over her head, most likely disrupting the sleek ponytail she'd made to catch all the flyaways. Midwest humidity had made its presence known already, and it wasn't officially summer yet. She'd blame the blush that surely crept up her neck at the moment on the heat wave too.

"A leaf, or a...a...blossom."

Of course. She'd fought the blossoms all morning. It was as if her mother had been cultivating wild honeysuckle in the beds instead of her usual day lilies and zinnias.

By now, he'd half risen from the booth to pick it out of her hair. She instinctively moved away, but her awkward step back only caught her off balance. Mark's hand was on her arm in an instant to steady her.

They looked down in unison at his hand wrapped around her forearm.

"Careful. Monte might boot you for manhandling the wait-staff." Janie said it with a smile, but she couldn't be more serious.

Mark dropped the little white flower next to the dish of creamers as evidence and sat again. A shadow crossed his face, but he glanced at the menu again to hide the expression. He probably wasn't expecting to be treated like an ordinary customer.

What was she supposed to do, roll out the welcome mat?

Fall into his arms and beg for a do-over?

No, thank you.

Mark shut the menu and turned over his mug for her to fill. "You know what? Surprise me. I'm out of practice," he said. Mark pulled out his phone and didn't give her another look.

She held the bottom of the carafe while she poured, lest Mark notice her hand shaking. Monte was so going to get an earful for this.

Chapter Three

Mark swirled a spoon in his coffee, thinking about the creative, painful ways he might punish Monte for this underhanded deed. Throwing Janie and him together without a hint that either one of them was back in town was just plain rotten. He'd glanced a few times toward the kitchen, but Monte was quick. Too guilty to look him in the eye, Monte busied himself with work behind the window, the coward that he was.

Meanwhile, Janie acted like he was little more than a stranger. She buzzed about the dining room, wiping tables, delivering orders, and taking payments. And going out of her way *not* to make eye contact considering he'd raised his finger three times without catching her attention. This pained him. The demise of their relationship was still fresh after all this time. It swam to the surface as soon as they'd faced each other.

Minutes later, Janie stopped by his booth to refill his mug. Eyes on the coffee streaming into his cup, definitely not on him.

"What did you decide to feed me?" He tried to keep his tone light, but it came out sounding forced and too chipper.

Janie's scowl pulled down the corners of her mouth. "French toast," she said flatly.

Oh.

"The perfect breakfast food, don't you think?" she asked. A darting glance. A one-sided grin. Then she moved on to the next table.

He chuckled under his breath. "That's a subjective statement," he said to himself.

During one of his more memorable visits to the cafe, Janie wanted to know why he'd ordered everything on the menu over the years except French toast. Monte's diner didn't offer a very big menu, so avoiding French toast when he'd tried everything else was obvious. Pancakes, yes. Waffles too. But French toast? Nope.

So he'd shared his woeful French toast story. A longtime girlfriend broke up with him over French toast. The dish had left a bad taste in his mouth. Not long after sharing that detail, he and Janie had started dating.

That nugget of nostalgia made his throat squeeze shut. He suddenly missed how she'd park herself in the booth opposite him if the diner wasn't busy. While he ate, Janie would talk his ear off, skipping from one random subject to the next with ease. Breakfast food trivia. Buying a miter saw. Stargazing on her sister's tour boat. Her cat's penchant for clawing the legs of a new sofa. He took a sip of his coffee, hoping to mask the feelings which were surely playing across his face like the all-is-lost scene in a romance flick.

He'd just have to come out and say what he came to say even if it wasn't his style. Janie appreciated a direct approach. And he'd wasted enough time.

In the kitchen, Monte tapped the bell to signal another

order was ready. His friend ducked his head, still avoiding eye contact. *We'll talk soon enough, my friend.*

Seconds later, Janie slid a plate of French toast garnished with strawberries in front of him. A dispenser of syrup too.

"Do you need anything else?" She scanned the dining room over her shoulder as she asked.

"Can you sit down for a minute?" The diner was clearing out. She'd sat with him before when it was much busier.

"I really can't." Janie clamped down on her lips while looking at his plate.

"Then can we talk after your shift?"

"I've got...an appointment after work."

He lifted his brows at the obvious lie. "Then how about I call you later?"

"I don't think so." She turned around, stopped, then faced him again.

"Are you the one who's been calling me and not leaving a message?" she asked.

"I...I wanted to let you know I was coming back to town in case you were here too."

Janie narrowed her eyes for several seconds, then gave an abrupt nod. The scrutiny almost made him squirm.

"I have to get back to work. If I'm busy, Billie will check you out." Janie turned on her heels and beelined it back into the kitchen.

This isn't going to be easy.

Mark sighed. He picked up his fork, cut into the French toast, and took the first bite. Monte did make the best French toast, bad breakups aside. It practically melted on his tongue. But even Monte's best culinary efforts couldn't make anything palatable today. The act of eating felt robotic. *Fork to French toast. French toast to mouth. Chew. Swallow. Repeat.*

While he polished off the late breakfast, his attention wandered to the scene outside the window. Main Street in Port Chance looked like the central thoroughfare of most small American towns which had experienced an influx of tax dollars and ambitious, young entrepreneurs. He knew this because he'd traveled the country for most of the last few years, writing features about these communities for *Backroads and Byways* magazine.

In Port Chance, storefronts built in a myriad of architectural styles from different eras stood side by side. Some were bare of ornamental features, while others were dressed with awnings, sherbet-colored painted doors, flower boxes with hip-sounding names like Daily Grind Coffee and Dough Baby Bakery. The beautification committee had taken donations for the welcome flags, which waved from the ornate street lamps, and for the enormous green pots overflowing with red petunias, Gerber daisies, lobelia, and sweet potato vines, adding a sense of unity to the downtown. From his viewpoint in Monte's diner, the calm presence of the Mississippi River flowed beyond the buildings and behind a small, grassy levy where Canada geese gathered and an occasional biker zipped past on a paved path.

He zeroed in on the little antique shop across the street, John's Shoppe of Curious Goods. John "Jumpin'" Goodwin, the grizzled owner, sat in his usual spot on a wooden bench painted banana yellow. His black lab with cataract-clouded eyes lay on the sidewalk beside him.

So much has changed, yet some things remained the same.

When Mark worked for the ad department at the newspaper, he'd stop for breakfast at Monte's place first on Fridays to get the ad proofs checked, then wander over to Jumpin's place. The shop held a hodgepodge of rustic furniture, antiques, and discarded knickknacks. An occasional treasure hid in the organized chaos of Jumpin's shop, like the sleeve of Cardinals baseball cards from the 1967 World Series team he'd found on one of his visits.

Mark swirled the last bite around his plate, soaking up the remnants of syrup. Good on her word, Janie stayed busy, so Mark paid his tab with Billie. He felt Janie's eyes on him the whole time while she sat in an empty booth rolling silverware into napkins. He lifted his chin in her direction as he made his way to the door, but she pretended not to notice.

* * *

Outside, the air smelled sweet, a combination of fresh-cut grass and the lilacs which bloomed in the narrow, green space between the diner and Herrold's Soda and Sweet Emporium next door. Jumpin' gave him a hearty wave when he spotted Mark on the sidewalk.

At least someone is happy to see me again.

Jumpin' had already pulled Mark's usual seat out from its hiding place behind the old pie safe by the time he crossed the street. The old, metal milk canister with a tractor seat attached to the top, uncomfortable as all get out, was a welcome sight. Besides, it was the thought that counted.

"What do you know today?" Jumpin' asked as if he'd seen him only yesterday instead of three years ago. His voice crackled like radio static. The sound made Mark want to clear his throat.

"Not much except that I ate too much." He undid the bottom-most button on his shirt before he sat. Sure enough, the canister wobbled underneath Mark's weight until he steadied it against the wall.

"Not hard to do at Monte's. He put this new thing on the menu"—he tapped his chin, looking up at the porch roof—"can't think of what he named it at the moment. But Texas toast, sausage gravy, Lorch's cheese. And the spice combination? Outta this world." He kissed his fingers and made a smacking sound with his lips.

"Monte knows how to come up with the crowd pleasers." He squinted to see through the diner window across the street, but the sun's glare was too strong. She was in there somewhere, maybe staring right back at him for all he knew. "So, how have you been?"

Jumpin' scratched his jaw. "Oh, you know. Been busy doing nothing, same as always."

"Has business been good?" Mark looked over his shoulder through the streaked window.

"Busy enough that I have to catch my breath talking the customers' ears off, I guess." He looked down at his dog who lay sprawled out on the porch floor. "Isn't that right, Wally?"

Wally lifted his head an inch off the floor and thumped his tail once in acknowledgement.

"Is it a coincidence that your Janie Wendell is back in town or is that serendipity at play?" Jumpin' leaned forward far enough to slap him on the knee.

"She's not my Janie," he said softly, ignoring the sideways smirk Jumpin' wore. "And it's just coincidence."

"Some would call it fate." He leaned over to brush at the top of his boot. Wally opened his eyes, licked his lips, then fell back into his semi-coma, complete with guttural snores and an occasional whole-body twitch.

"Did you fare okay through the flood?" he asked, eager to move on from Jumpin's line of questioning.

"Better than the Yellow Pier." He looked down the hill toward the bottom of Main Street. The flood waters hadn't touched many of the businesses at this part of the main thoroughfare through Port Chance. Farther west, where Main Street dipped and the levy wasn't as high, the river took over. The Yellow Pier restaurant suffered the worst of it.

Mark knew the restaurant well. He'd rented the studio apartment above the restaurant from the owner, Thomas Hicklebourne, for a year after he'd quit selling advertising for the *River City Times*. It had been tiny, and a water spot on the bathroom ceiling dripped during heavy rain. Many a night he'd studied the crack running up the plaster on his bedroom wall and wondered if the building would be split in half when he woke the next morning, and he'd open his eyes to see the sky. But cracked plaster and leaky roofs aside, he'd been close to Janie. That's all that had counted. And now he was back there in the same little apartment until he could find more permanent housing. Thomas joked he'd been holding it for him for three years now.

"I hear there's going to be a town-wide clean-up this weekend. You gonna stick around for that?" Jumpin' asked. "Can't say I'll be of much use, but I suppose offering some moral support wouldn't be turned away."

"I'll be around."

"What are you up to these days? Still writing on the road?" Jumpin' asked. He pulled a metal camp cup from the primitive wooden pie safe beside him and held his thermos poised over the empty cup. "Coffee?"

"No thanks. Had my fill." Jumpin's coffee could revive the dead.

Jumpin' shrugged, set the cup out of sight again, and refilled his own mug.

"I've taken a job at the Iowa Travel and Recreation Bureau in Davenport. They're publishing some new guides."

"So, it's permanent?"

"It is. Or, I think so?"

"You're not feeling the wanderlust anymore?"

Mark looked down at his feet. He wouldn't call it wanderlust, taking the travel writing job for the magazine. But it had been his first real break for a career change after slogging away selling advertising for the *River City Times*. In the back of his mind, he'd always been a writer. But advertising paid the bills. He'd been good at it. It was only after he'd sold his first article that he'd really believed he could make a living freelancing, and if he was lucky, a staff writer down the road. He almost laughed, thinking about that now. One little restaurant review, and suddenly he'd felt like he could walk into *The New Yorker* and land a staff writer position. Janie had given him so much encouragement in the early months of their relationship. But once the magazine opportunity materialized, it all went downhill from there.

"I'm right where I belong now."

Jumpin' leaned over, sloshing coffee from his mug across his pant leg, but he didn't seem to mind. He gave Mark's knee a hearty slap.

"That's good to hear, son. We like having you around here."

Mark's first thought was Janie when Jumpin' said "we." But then Mark realized he'd only meant Wally. The dog lifted his shaggy head to reposition himself under Jumpin's hand when he scratched Wally's ear.

They sat there in comfortable silence watching cars inch past. Mark's attention was drawn to the windows of Daisy Gap Cafe again but all he could see was the reflection of this side of the street in the daylight-tinged windows.

"I'm going take a look around." He rose after casting another glance toward the cafe. Even when Janie's shift was over, she'd be leaving through the back door. There was zero chance she had plans to see him again today anyway. She'd made that perfectly clear.

"I haven't taken anything in lately that might interest you," Jumpin' said with a shrug. "Then again, stuff sometimes just shows up."

"Maybe my tastes have changed over the last three years."

Jumpin' snorted. "And maybe they haven't. Say, where you living now?"

Mark stopped over the threshold. When he arrived back in town, his old apartment above the restaurant was still available. His landlord told him it had been vacant for a while and it needed a good scrubbing, but he could have it if he wanted. Downstairs, the Yellow Pier's condition was a different story.

"I'm back above the restaurant."

Jumpin' grimaced. "That place is going to have a mold problem if it doesn't already."

"So far, so good."

"I've got an extra couch if you need it," Jumpin' offered. "Adelia is claiming the other bedroom next weekend for a visit, but she won't mind if I have a houseguest."

"That's all right, but thanks. I've got everything I need."

Jumpin' and Wally followed him into the shop. Mark

blinked a few times, letting his eyes adjust to the dim space after sitting in the lemonade light of midday. He smiled the instant the familiar smell hit him—wood smoke, tobacco, and something floral—the last of which he could never find its origin.

Overhead, the same rusty light fixtures swung with the gentle breeze floating in through the open front door. There was never any rhyme or reason to the layout of the store, but now that Mark thought about it, the big pieces dictated where everything else landed. There was the immense European wardrobe with an awful refinish job. A two-seater sleigh with tattered maroon upholstery. One marble-topped, twelve-foot-long credenza which Jumpin' proudly had noted came from a Scottish castle. How the piece ended up in an antique shop in eastern Iowa was a story Jumpin' never explained despite Mark's prodding.

More furniture created a serpentine path through the long, narrow store, sometimes blocking an aisle so retracing one's steps to get to another part of the room was necessary. And a sundry of objects lay on every flat surface, or were hung, draped, or tucked into open doors and drawers, thus tempting shoppers to take in every detail or risk missing something of monumental importance.

Mark stopped in front of a faded walnut desk. Sunbeams cut through the circular window near the apex of the ceiling and across the shop, bathing the desk in light while highlighting the dust eddies swirling in the air. A set of four milky hobnail juice glasses rested on the fold-down desktop held in place by rusted chains. An old photo album opened to a page with stoic, unsmiling people in nineteenth-century dress caught his eye for a minute. He flipped through a few pages, looking at faces for no reason other than the inexplicable need to give these strangers more than a passing glance.

Next to it, Mark scanned a coat tree loaded with straw hats, a gray, satin-lined fedora, and ball caps with seed company logos. He plucked the fedora from its hook, settled it on his head, and checked his reflection in the wavy glass of an oval mirror behind him.

A sense of déjà vu hit him. Janie standing beside him in an antique shop in Galena, smiling as he fiddled with a hat on his head like this one.

I'm getting Marlon Brando vibes, she'd teased.

I'd rather you get Mark Christie vibes, he'd countered.

The memory of the way she slipped her arm through his and pulled him close burned in the pit of his stomach. They'd kissed without caring who came across them huddled in the darkened corner, sandwiched between a hulking shelf stacked with musty-smelling books and a faceless mannequin wearing a faux fur coat.

He swiped the triggering object off his head. *No good*.

As he took in the myriad of discarded knickknacks and once-treasured heirlooms, his thoughts wandered to his mother. She'd been gone almost twenty-five years now. Muriel passed on her love of old things to him. Saturdays had been their day to explore. Mark could still feel the tickle of excitement he had as a boy waking up in anticipation of a day of uninterrupted attention from his mother. Their day would begin with pancakes at IHOP, followed by visiting the list of antique shops his mother handed over to him as soon as they were on their way. Dubuque, Burlington, and all the little towns in between on the Great River Road. His mother never strayed too far east or west of the Mississippi, almost as if she were afraid she'd lose her way without the river for guidance.

His reminiscing was interrupted when a walking stick, propped against a wash basin cabinet, caught his eye.

Mark picked it up and inspected it closely. Worn leather wrapped the curved handle. A black rubber tip protected the other end. But in between, where the burnished wood caught the glint from the light overhead, primitive carvings decorated the surface from the grip all the way down to the rubber cap. Stick-straight trees, flowers, a cabin, and four-legged creatures of the forest wound their way from top to bottom, all connected by a dotted path.

Frowning, he turned it over in his hands.

What would I do with someone's old walking stick?

He tapped the rubber tip on the floor.

Nothing, that's what. Mark replaced the stick where he'd found it.

No matter how many times Mark roamed the nooks of Jumpin's place, he'd always found something intriguing. But today was different. A melancholy had settled inside him, something that offered no room for whatever objects he came across here. He made his way back to Jumpin' who'd settled on his creaky stool behind the old apothecary display counter.

"I told you I didn't have anything for you," Jumpin' said.

Mark tapped on the counter on his way past.

"I guess sometimes I need to see for myself."

Chapter Four

Two mornings later, Janie sat at her kitchen table, sipping coffee and wearing a ratty sweatshirt zipped up to her neck with its hood pulled over her head. She shivered. Distracted, she'd forgotten to close the windows before bedtime, and the late-spring air took the liberty of cooling off the house overnight. She'd awoken, freezing, at five o'clock despite the sheet, fleece blanket, and Mimi's log cabin quilt layered over her. Insulated for all seasons, the cozy little house warmed up in a hurry when she lit the wood stove. But she'd mistakenly thought May in east-central Iowa meant wood stove season was over.

Janie clutched the little black mug with both hands, hoping to warm her hands. The Two Tree Coffee logo on the side of the cup was a bittersweet reminder of the life she'd left behind in Minnesota. It was a parting gift from Cora Martin, her librarian friend, when she'd left Hendricks. She missed Cora and their sporadic yet comforting chats. Cora's high-energy personality matched her own. She'd also listened when Janie needed it most, especially in the early months of Janie's breakup with

Mark. Janie shuddered thinking about that dark time again. But like she did with all things unpleasant, Janie quickly tucked the memory away into the back corner of her mind where it would stay until something or someone reminded her what she tried desperately to forget.

Mark.

Janie pushed on the skin between her eyebrows, willing herself to put him out of her mind. Darn that Monte for keeping secrets. She'd felt out of sorts ever since Mark showed his face in the cafe. Her boss was still deftly avoiding fessing up to his crime.

The little slant of light poking through the crack between the curtains warmed the skin on her hand. Janie stood to push back the curtains so the sunshine could light every corner of her tiny kitchen. A flash of blue cruised past her line of vision in the driveway, the sound of squeaky brakes cutting through the silence. Seconds later, Kit Wendell rapped sharply on her door before barging in. Her youngest sister had never had a problem making her presence known.

"It's eight thirty already, and you're still in pajamas," Kit said heading straight for the Tupperware filled with cookies Janie had baked the night before. Kit snapped the lid open, rummaged around in the container, and came away with two oatmeal chocolate chip cookies—one for her mouth and another for back up.

"Did you come here to pick on me, or do you need something important?" She pushed out a chair with her foot, a signal for Kit to sit. Janie noted a few silver strands peppering Kit's hair near her temples. *How can my baby sister be graying already?* It was inevitable, she knew, but Janie still couldn't quite believe she was only three years shy of turning forty herself.

Kit plopped down. "The latter. Mom has a doctor's appointment today, and I'm busy."

"My shift starts before the lunch hour, Kit. Why am I learning about this now? She didn't say anything to me."

Her sister held a finger up while she chewed. A stall tactic. Kit couldn't care less about decorum.

"A crew is coming to rebuild the dock and the ticket stand this morning. In fact, they're here now. I said I'd take her, but I need to be here. They've needed a lot of handholding already. I don't trust them."

"C'mon, Kit. It's my first full week back to work, and you want me to put Monte in a bind with less than two hours' notice?"

"He loves you. He'll understand." Kit lifted her shoulder nonchalantly. The second cookie disappeared in a flash.

Monte would make it work if Janie begged off for two hours. She wasn't a slacker; he knew that. "That's not the point."

Kit pushed away from the table and decided to explore the contents of Janie's refrigerator. While she inspected the packaged cheeses and popped a strawberry into her mouth, Janie debated on asking Kit something. Kit settled on a jar of jam, closed the refrigerator, and caught Janie studying her.

"What?" she asked.

Janie couldn't think of a roundabout way to ask so she settled on her usual approach.

"What do you know about Mark being back in town?"

Kit made a face after she dipped a finger in the lingonberry jam.

"What is this stuff?" Kit hurried to the sink and spit. She turned on the faucet, rinsing her mouth in the stream of water.

Janie swept the jar off the counter and into the trash. "Never mind. Answer me."

Kit wiped her mouth with the back of her hand. "I don't know. Ask him."

"Have you seen him before today?"

"Off and on. He worked on an article about me running the boat up to Dubuque for the opening weekend." Kit frowned. "I thought you weren't interested in him?"

"They must have been VIP boat passengers to garner an article."

Kit waved away the implication. "Just some politician types. I mean, he isn't in town as frequently as when you two were..." Kit pulled a frown. "Sorry."

Janie sighed. It didn't bother her, Kit bringing up their past. What bothered her was people expecting her to still be upset about it.

"It's okay. I'm just curious."

"I mean, he and Monte are friends. And Jumpin' and Mark, they're a pair too."

Janie laughed. She couldn't picture it. If there were ever two polar opposites, it would be Mark and Jumpin' Goodwin.

"How long is he planning to stay?" Janie kept her tone light.

Kit opened the refrigerator on the hunt for something else. "Again, I'm not Mark's confidante. You'll have to ask him." She shut the door when nothing piqued her interest and turned to Janie. "Why are you so curious if you're not interested?"

Janie looked into her mug and shook her head. "No reason."

Kit made a sound like she didn't believe her. Then, "So you'll take Mom this morning?"

It sounded like she didn't have a choice. Hopefully Monte wouldn't grumble too much.

Janie's phone buzzed on the table next to her. Rose's name popped onto the screen. A second later, she was calling.

"I figured a call would work much faster," her oldest sister reasoned when Janie answered. "Is Kit there?"

"Yeah, just got here." She met Kit's eyes, and Kit gave an exaggerated eye roll. Rose and Kit clashed more often than not. Order and chaos, those two.

"I said I'd take care of it," Kit said, raising her voice so Rose would hear. "I asked her if she'd take Mom first," she then said to Janie in a hushed tone.

"I'm taking her, Rose. No worries." Janie sometimes found herself between Rose and Kit when they butted heads.

Rose sighed. In the background, chickens squawked. Janie smiled.

"I keep meaning to have you out to dinner, but this crazy schedule of ours, it's ridiculous," Rose said. "Maybe Sunday or Monday?"

Janie chuckled. "I'll have to check *my* crazy schedule." Aside from working at the diner and pulling honeysuckle around her parents' property, she was free.

"I'll get back to you," Rose said. "It's so good to have you back. And thanks for taking Mom today."

"You're welcome. See you soon."

When Janie looked up, Kit sat slumped against her seat, wearing a forlorn expression.

"What's wrong?"

"Rose. She hates me."

Janie snorted. "Listen to yourself. Rose does not hate you. She's just hyper organized. Fastidious."

"And I'm not."

Janie shrugged. "We all have our gifts."

Kit sat up straight and rubbed her thighs. "Yeah? What's mine?"

"Seriously?"

"I am." Kit huffed when Janie shook her head. "What's wrong with wanting to hear what you think? I mean, obviously Rose is perfect," she said with an air of sarcasm. "You're a ball of energy and always upbeat. Sadie is as loyal as a Labrador. What am I?"

"You're a fountain of knowledge."

"Right." Kit laughed, but Janie could tell that answer pleased Kit. "How so?"

"You know a little bit about everything. You're very capable."

It wasn't a stretch. Kit could change out a faucet, the oil on her car, and name all the flowers and shrubs along the shoreline from here to the river's head at Lake Itasca. She'd made her way from one coast to another multiple times, first as a long-haul truck driver right out of community college, then as a team transport member of a dog rescue group based in Des Moines. She'd been a bit of a vagabond in her twenties, something Janie admired only because she wished she were more like her sister—spontaneous, carefree, and confident. Janie was told she possessed some of those same qualities, but she knew better. It was all for show.

Kit nodded, still smiling a little. She dropped her gaze to her lap. "I really am sorry for dropping the Mom Bomb on you. I'll make it up. Promise."

"I don't mind taking her. That's what I came back for, Kit. For the family stuff."

"It really is nice having you home."

"I'm glad to be here."

And for a minute Janie didn't think about why she'd come back to Port Chance or why she left in the first place. It was as if her town, her family and her job had been counting the months for her return, forgiving her for the lengthy absence, no questions asked.

Later that morning, Janie straightened herself in the uncomfortable chair in the doctor's office. Her mom sat next to her, arms crisscrossed and resting in her lap, her head supported by the wall behind them, eyes closed. She was the picture of calm.

"Are you in pain?" You never knew with Sonya. Her mother was as even-keeled as Janie's younger sister.

"No pain at all." Sonya laid a hand on Janie's knee. "I can feel your foot bouncing and our chairs aren't even touching,"

Janie uncrossed her legs. "Sorry. I just really hate these places."

Sonya leaned forward and looked at her. "Everything will be fine."

The IV taped to her mother's arm, making her skin pucker where the needle slipped through her skin, told a different story. That familiar sick feeling in the pit of her stomach coursed through Janie again.

"You're too nonchalant about this whole thing."

Sonya huffed. "And you're too much of a doomsayer. I feel

great. I even ate eggs and sausage this morning and didn't actually feel sick afterward." Sonya looked at her. "Thank you for caring about me, but I'll be okay."

Janie pursed her lips together and nodded. She wasn't buying it, though. Her mother still wore the PICC line longer than the doctor had predicted. It'd been ten days longer, in fact.

Her thoughts were interrupted by a rap on the door. It opened before either of them acknowledged it with a "come in." Rhett Farr burst into the room with a wide grin and stopped like he waited for a round of applause.

Janie almost groaned. Why hadn't it occurred to her their paths might cross now that Sonya had been assigned to another doctor after her long-time physician just retired?

And of course if *had* to be Rhett Farr. Former class president. Peaked in popularity senior year in high school by being voted Most Likely to Go Places. He'd stayed in Port Chance since his family's roots were imbedded the deepest of anyone living in town or lying in Pilot Hill Cemetery. He'd been trying to impress her since sixth grade with sweets he pulled out of his lunch sack. Rhett was an attention hog and still in love with himself.

"Hi, ladies."

"Rhett," Janie said flatly. Next to her, Sonya's brow creased when she heard the tone in Janie's voice.

"How are you feeling, Sonya?" He asked this while his eyes roved over Janie. *Insufferable.*

"I'm well, considering this," she said, lifting her arm onto the small, built-in table next to where she sat. He rolled up on a squeaky stool, put his glasses on, and gently probed the site with his fingers.

"No redness. That's good," he said, now all business, thank goodness.

He lowered Sonya's arm down and directed her to the examination table where he rolled the leg of her capri pants past her knee so he could undress the wound. Janie got one peek at the half-moon-shaped gash on her mother's shin, then studied the skin cancer identification poster on the wall until the bandage was changed. If the day ever came that she had children, Janie didn't know how she'd survive the blood and needles stuff.

"So, can this be taken out any time soon?" Sonya asked, nodding to the IV.

Janie knew the answer was "no" even before he spoke. He wouldn't look either of them in the eye while he spread his hands out on his knees and studied the floor.

"I think we need to give it awhile longer," he said. Rhett rose to stand over the tiny sink in the corner to wash his hands.

Sonya's wide-eyed, hopeful expression fell until she found Janie watching her. She answered with a reassuring smile.

"I suppose the good news is that I get to come back to see you lovely people more," she quipped. Her mother wasn't short in the sarcasm department at least.

"I might put in a referral to someone in Iowa City. There's a specialist there who might help knock this out a little faster than what we're capable of here."

Rhett's face was grimmer than Janie expected when he turned around again. A minute ago he'd been flirting with her in plain sight of Sonya.

Janie sat up straighter. "Is something wrong?"

"No," he said. "Not yet anyway. Just playing it safe."

Janie walked side by side with her mother back to the car. Sonya paused before she opened the passenger door.

"It'll be fine, honey. You'll see."

"You heard what he said. People go to Iowa City for serious stuff."

"It's a university hospital system. Top notch. Dr. Farr just wants to kick it to the curb once and for all." She lifted her leg to peer down at the fresh bandage peeking out from under her pant leg. "That doesn't sound like a bad plan, does it?"

Janie walked around to the driver's side. She wished she had her mother's sunny outlook. She'd been told she did on numerous occasions, and maybe once upon a time she had, but trusting the universe that a good disposition and faith made everything work out wasn't realistic.

She knew that from experience.

Chapter Five

Mark slowed to a walk along the bike path after logging an effortless five miles early Saturday morning. A breeze tinged with the warmth coming later in the day caressed his face and cooled the sweat on his skin. To his left, sunlight cast jewels on the Mississippi. Something broke the water's surface behind the veil of cattails that lined the bank.

He focused on his breathing, which matched the rhythm of a bullfrog croaking nearby. It felt good to be running again. Still, he had a long way from being capable of the half marathon he hoped to run in October in Dubuque's Fall Run Under the Sun. He'd started out in March, in terrible running shape, determined to get back at it. It was a resolution of sorts, two months late. His newly minted goal coincided with his decision to return to Port Chance. New beginnings and all that.

Up ahead, Kit Wendell's tour boat bobbed dockside at Love's Landing. The captain herself wasn't in sight, but it was still early. If he remembered right, weekend tours didn't start until nine o'clock. Kit was a lot like Janie—energetic, a little mouthy, funny. He got along well with her. But whereas Kit was borderline anti-social, which he found funny for someone who served the public, Janie's life-of-the-party personality could revive a morgue. He smiled. They'd been a good mix, her rock-n-roll persona to his mellow-jazz demeanor.

He stopped to stretch his quads then pulled the towel from his waistband to wipe his brow. The back of the Daisy Gap Cafe drew his attention a block away. Was she tending to the break-fast crowd? Would she be working the dinner hour instead? He couldn't keep eating there, hoping to catch a minute of her attention. His bank account couldn't take dining out seven days a week.

Footsteps sounded behind him.

"Mark?"

It took him a few seconds to put a name to the woman who jogged up to him. The short, auburn bob, pulled back into a small ponytail, emphasized the high cheekbones and cleft chin that connected her to her father.

Adelia Goodwin. Jumpin's daughter.

"I thought that was you," she said when she stopped. "I didn't expect to see you again for a while, the traveling jour-nalist that you are."

"Change of plans. Life on the road didn't suit me after all."

"I'm all for big life changes," she said with a shrug. "So are you settled here again?"

He nodded toward the other end of town. "I'm in the apart-ment above the Yellow Pier."

Adelia grimaced. "Oh. I'm sorry."

"Don't be. I moved in after the water receded. And since it's on the second floor, I'm high and dry." He laughed at her expression, which told him she wasn't so sure about his decision to stay there. "The owner knocked a couple hundred off the rent citing an 'environmental discount.'"

She snorted. "The least they could do for the possibility of contracting some mold-related illness." She pointed ahead toward the bike path. "Want to walk for a bit and catch up?"

"Sure. And I'll be fine, encroaching mold aside. So, visiting your dad?"

Adelia nodded. "He's downsizing. If you've seen his shop, you can imagine what his house looks like." Her eyes bugged.

"A herculean task, I'm sure."

"I wish Cash was able to make it, but he couldn't get away from work. Maybe soon," she said.

"I've never met your brother. He must not make it back that often."

She wrinkled her nose. "He and Dad butt heads a lot. They're both stubborn."

Jumpin' stubborn? *Nah.*

They'd walked past the glass studio, a little Victorian with gingerbread trim. He'd often thought it a miniature version of the Wendells' house. Maybe the same person built both houses —very much a possibility in these small towns. The tracks were up ahead where the path snaked below a monstrous, wooden trestle. Trains crossed the Mississippi here.

"If you need an extra set of muscles, let me know," he said. "Your dad is such a character."

Adelia stopped. She grinned, holding his gaze a little longer than she ever had before now. "I might have to take you up on that."

Mark looked back the way they'd come. "I should get back. A deadline looms."

"Of course," she said with a firm nod.

They walked in silence for a bit, listening to the sounds of birds along the river singing their morning songs. A breeze picked up, drying the damp hair on Mark's neck. He needed a haircut. The ends were starting to curl.

"Do you have plans to stay in Port Chance indefinitely?" Adelia asked.

"I'm looking for a more permanent place. Depends on what I find."

"You certainly have enough furnishings to fill up whatever place you buy."

"It might be too much."

Adelia clucked her tongue. "Even after all these years, I still can't believe the audacity of your stepfather, thinking he could sell everything right out from under you without asking."

"It didn't surprise me in the least. I haven't seen him since the summer my mom died."

"I'm sorry," she said.

"I'm not. He never cared for me."

"You have her belongings now. That's all that matters."

They walked on. Mark's thoughts turned to what his mother left behind.

He'd been renting a storage unit from Adelia in Davenport for longer than he could remember. Their mutual love of old things brought them together when he and his mother wandered into Adelia's antique shop back when Muriel Christie was still alive twenty-five years ago. Adelia was older than him by at least ten years, but her youthful vigor now hid it well. She'd tracked him down at college when Mark's stepfather started unloading his late wife's heirloom-quality furniture. Adelia had recognized much of it since it had come from her shop. *Doesn't Mark want any of it back?* she'd asked. According to Mark's stepfather, he'd asked Mark, but his stepson turned it all down. It wasn't until years later he'd learned Adelia paid his stepfather outright for the furniture, turning it over to Mark without asking for a dime. It had sat in her storage unit ever since.

He'd met Jumpin' through Adelia around that time too.

"I'll take it off your hands in the near future. Promise."

"I don't worry about that. You'll get it in good time," she said. Adelia paused while she cleared her throat. "And I imagine you and Janie ...?"

"No, we're not...no."

Adelia frowned. "I thought you two were yin and yang."

Was everyone in town going to make him rehash their broken relationship?

"Didn't work out."

"I'm sorry," she said, though her chipper tone said otherwise.

Sometimes he got the feeling Adelia was attracted to him. It was never close to mutual, but she'd been so kind to him over the years he was careful to not encourage her in any way. Mark liked to think of her as an older sister—someone who had his back. But something seemed to have changed since the last time he saw her.

"It was a long time ago."

"Though sometimes certain people are here to stay." Adelia pressed her hand to her chest while studying him with intensity.

"Sometimes," he mused.

It was a good thing they'd arrived back at the point where they'd part ways. What he assumed was her car was the only one in the little parking lot in front of Love's Landing. He couldn't wait to get back to his apartment to shower. The heat of the day was rising now that the sun moved from behind the trees.

Adelia hugged him suddenly, catching him by surprise. He remembered that about her. She was a hugger.

"It was so good to see you, Mark. Maybe we can get coffee or...lunch sometime. I'm sure there's a lot more to catch up on."

There was no doubt in Mark's mind that Adelia wanted something more than just a catch-up coffee date. As she got into her car, his attention drifted past her and across the green space on Water Street to the back entrance to the Daisy Gap Cafe. Only this time, Janie sat there on the low wall outside the blue back door, legs crossed, one foot swinging.

And this time she stared right back at him.

Chapter Six

Monte closed the restaurant after the lunch rush on Sundays. He also didn't open Mondays, which gave Janie a much-needed break.

"Are you headed down to the gazebo like everyone else in town?" Monte asked. He worked over the griddle, giving it a good scrubbing while it was still warm.

"It's the place to be today, right?" She'd driven past the Yellow Pier restaurant after hearing about the flood damage. The only indication from the outside that the river had ripped through the restaurant was the faint, mud-tinged water line ringing the building at window level.

"I'm heading down there myself after I drop Camilla off at home."

"I've decided to come too." Camilla had snuck up behind Janie, her soft footsteps not registering amid Monte's scraping.

"Are you sure, baby? You've been on your feet all morning," he said.

"Positive."

Camilla walked up behind Monte and hugged him around the middle. He set his tool aside and wrapped his arms around her in return.

Janie smiled at the two even though she wondered if Camilla's affectionate display was more a show of claiming Monte as hers in front of Janie. Camilla was a hard read. It might take another week or two before Camilla warmed up to her.

Janie untied her apron as she walked over to the time card rack. "Your wedding invite came today, by the way. Count me in." They'd be married in early July at Larkspur Park by the river. The event barn at Apple Hill Orchard would host the reception.

"That's so good to hear," Camilla said, a genuine smile now lighting her face. "I'm sure time will fly between now and then, but it seems like the day is taking forever to get here."

Monte rolled his eyes. "I, for one, can't wait. Flower arrangements have taken over my garage."

Camilla gently elbowed his ribs with a laugh. "So not true. And it was your idea we use it to organize."

"Only because you wanted to use the basement. And I can't watch Luke's games with all the yakking." He thumbed in Camilla's direction. "She and her sister, big talkers."

His fiancée giggled. Janie smiled at Camilla's delight. Her smiles tended to look forced, but not today. The two were ridiculously in love, and it made Janie happy. Monte deserved it. He'd been such a force of good for the community for so long.

"Did Monte tell you his brother is coming all the way from Portugal to take over Monte's kitchen for the rehearsal dinner?" Camilla asked.

"What a sweet brother he must be."

"Oh, nononono. I *begged* him to come is more like it," Monte said, holding his head in his hands. "You know why? Mark volunteered to oversee the dinner, that's why. No one wants Mark Christie cooking dinner for thirty-plus people."

The smile felt pasted on her face. Janie coughed into her hand, an involuntary reflex at hearing Mark would be at the rehearsal dinner too. Of course he'd be there. He and Monte were best friends. But the news caught her off guard. She had to compose herself before the big day, a must-do as crucial as finding a dress for the occasion.

Monte's squinty look when she turned back to him made her pause. She still hadn't called out Monte's trick the other day —him sending her out into the dining room without mentioning the man responsible for breaking her heart was waiting to order breakfast. Calling him out on it would imply she cared about Mark. And she didn't. It'd just surprised her is all.

"You don't suppose you'd want to help us with some little thing that day, would you?" Monte asked.

Janie didn't miss the stirring behind his gaze. He was up to something.

"Anything you want, Monte." She steeled herself.

"Can you bring the flower arrangements from the ceremony to the reception? There won't be too many," he asked.

"There will be six, I believe," Camilla said. "The table arrangements will already be at the reception. These will be the larger ones for the head table and foyer."

Shuffle flower arrangements? That didn't sound too threatening. She could handle it.

Janie nodded. "You bet."

Camilla clutched Monte's arm, looking up at him with an impish grin. "One more item to check off the list."

He shook his head and winked at Janie. "It's never-ending."

Monte still wore that look, though—a he's-got-something-up-his-sleeve look. Maybe wedding flowers were more dangerous than she imagined.

* * *

After filling out her time card, Janie retreated to her car parked out back. She balled up her apron, tossed it into the car, and changed into her olive-green galoshes while stewing over what Monte had up his sleeves.

Janie checked her reflection in the rearview mirror as she pulled the rubber band from her hair and held it between her teeth, finger combing the flyaway strands into another messy bun. No one she'd see during the next few hours would care how her hair looked. There were more important matters at hand.

A crowd had already gathered around the gazebo at the bottom of High Street as she made her way down the sloping sidewalk. Now that she had more time to take note, the damage the waters left behind was obvious. It had been a one-hundred-year flood, she'd heard someone say at the diner. Gone were the shrubs and flowers the beautification committee had planted last month. A distinct line of river mud coated the gazebo's brick foundation. Two metal railings had been torn away from the pillars. But the gazebo wasn't the focus of today's rehab efforts. It was the Yellow Pier restaurant.

"Where do we even start?" a woman muttered next to Janie when she stopped in front of where the mayor, Mona Jarvis, had planted herself on top of a picnic table. Volunteers gathered around, waiting for their marching orders.

Janie brushed hair away from her forehead. "Your guess is as good as mine."

"You're Janie Wendell, right?" the woman asked.

"I am. Sorry, you are?"

"Linn Miranelli." She stuck out her hand. "I know your sister Rose from the farm. I work there. You two look alike."

When Janie took Linn's hand, the strength behind the woman's handshake was surprising despite her small stature. Janie eyed Linn behind her sunglasses.

"There are so many new faces in town since I left three years ago. Have you been here long?"

Linn released her hand and balled her fist before dropping it to her side. "Only a few months," she said before startling slightly when Mayor Jarvis tapped the top of the picnic table with a broom handle to get everyone's attention.

"Thanks for coming out, everyone! We've got our work cut out for us today." Mayor Jarvis's throaty voice carried so well she didn't need a microphone. She held up three fingers. "There will be three teams. The movers, the shovelers, and the loaders."

It was the first town-wide work day as a result of the flood, posted on the city government's website by the mayor. As a fourth-generation Port Chance resident, Mona Jarvis excelled at rallying people together. Janie remembered her as the mom who took charge of the class parties, chaperoned field trips, and organized the after-prom party. Mona's daughter, Julie, had been class president, a take-charge person even at seventeen. The last Janie heard, Julie produced documentaries and lived in San Diego.

"Were you around when the river came through?" Linn asked.

"I wasn't."

"It was awful. Thank goodness someone beat me out of renting the apartment above the restaurant. I don't know what I would've done," Linn said.

"Where do you live?"

"At the small apartment building behind the medical office. It's not very big, but it's good enough for what I need. Sorry to hear about your mom, by the way."

Janie felt Mark's presence before she set eyes on him. Somehow, she knew exactly where he'd appear when he came around the other side of the gazebo. He scanned the crowd and paused for a few seconds when he noticed her. One corner of his mouth ticked up before he went back to taking in the scene around the mayor's makeshift stage. The skin on her bare arms pimpled with gooseflesh, and she rubbed them while cursing her body for betraying her.

Linn cleared her throat, bringing Janie back to earth. Linn had asked her a question.

"I...uh...sorry? I didn't catch what you said." Thank goodness for her sunglasses. Surely Mark couldn't tell she noticed him.

"Your mom," Linn said. "Rose has been keeping me up to date about her health."

"She'll pull through okay. You can't raise four girls without a little grit."

Linn shrank a little at the comment. If Janie wasn't so attuned to reading people, she wouldn't have noticed. Something in Linn's demeanor told Janie that she'd lived through something unpleasant.

Minutes later, everyone was asked to pick a group. Eyeing the tables, booths, and heavy kitchen equipment a crew had already brought outside, Janie had no intention of loading any of it onto the flatbed trailers parked up and down Main Street.

She spotted a group of shovels propped up outside the front door and grabbed one before they were all claimed. Janie headed into the dim confines of the Yellow Pier, far away from Mark. The mental image of him hugging the woman on the bike path the other day burned itself into her memory.

Out of sight, out of mind. It was the only cure for keeping Mark out of her thoughts.

Despite the floor fans set on high, Janie pulled the damp fabric of her shirt away from her chest where it was pasted after an hour's worth of work. But it was worse out in the sun. Through the front window, she caught glimpses of volunteers moving furniture on the flatbeds, their faces red with exertion. Mark was one of them. The gray tank he wore was soaked with sweat, a dark "V" stretching from his neck all the way down to his waist. His skin glistened in the sunlight, and when he stopped to wipe the sweat from his forehead with a navy bandana, she subconsciously mirrored him, running a hand across her forehead too.

Looking away, she stabbed at the layer of mud again with the shovel. How could she get that man out of her head if he was around every corner in this town? She still hadn't figured out why he'd come back to Port Chance of all places. There were plenty of places to live that weren't *here*.

"I thought I was seeing a ghost the other day when I walked into the exam room. Then I realized you've been haunting me every day since you left town."

Janie froze mid-shovel and turned. *She'd* haunted him?

51

Rhett Farr had been lurking around every corner since grade school.

"You didn't know I was back even though I've been here for weeks? In a small town like this? I don't believe it." She eased the shovel over the wheelbarrow and dumped it, a small plume of dust billowing upward. Rhett waved it away with a cross look before he put on his best smile again.

"It's been busy at the office. We're down a nurse and two assistants. If only I had a diner full of hungry people to feed instead of heal." He laughed.

Janie took a deep breath and faced him again. "Monte's down a waitperson. I'm sure that can be arranged if you're ready for a career change." She shot him a smile—one that felt as insincere as his looked.

Rhett grew serious. "I'd much prefer my salary to that of a waiter's."

"Less stress might be worth it."

He shook his head. "I enjoy making people well."

"Me too."

"Huh?"

"Same concept, different tools. You work with a stethoscope. My instruments are a fork and a spoon."

"Funny," he said flatly. "Enough intellectual sparring. I'm formally inviting you to sit with me during the barbecue at the end of the work day." He dabbed at the sweat beads above his lip with a bandana.

"I didn't plan to go to the barbecue. I have...other plans." That wasn't very convincing.

Rhett took her shovel and scooped two big loads into the wheelbarrow as if five seconds of chivalry might change her mind.

"But I want to hear about what you've been up to in Michigan for the last three years."

"Minnesota. I lived in Minnesota."

"That's right. I'd like to hear about it." He dumped another shovelful of caked mud into the wheelbarrow before Janie took the shovel back.

"Look, Rhett. I'm overwhelmed with my mom's situation, work, and being back here in general. I haven't really settled in yet. I don't really have much free time."

The dejected look on Rhett's face almost made her cave.

Rhett sighed loudly. "I know I can be a little...pushy sometimes. But I'd really like to take you out sometime. You know, now that you and Mike ..."

"Mark."

He nodded impatiently as if using the correct name of the guy she'd given her heart to for three years was beneath him. "...are over," he finished.

She shook her head. "I'm not interested, Rhett. Sorry."

Linn, who'd been working in the kitchen, walked past with a red handle in one hand and the rest of the shovel in the other. "That layer is like cement in there," she said. A splotch of mud punctuated her chin; another caked her cheek. "Do you think there's a shovel to spare outside?"

"Let me," said Rhett.

His focus turned so quickly from the date proposition to getting a replacement shovel for Linn that Janie laughed. Confusion clouded Linn's face. Rhett hurried back into the restaurant not thirty seconds later to present her with a green-handled shovel as if it was an engagement ring. It wouldn't surprise Janie if he'd wrestled it away from one of the other workers outside.

"I don't think we've met yet," Rhett said to Linn.

The guy was something. But if an introduction helped turn his attention away from her and onto Linn, she was all for it.

"Rhett. Linn. Linn. Rhett." There.

"*Dr.* Rhett Farr. It's a pleasure." He took Linn's hand, and for a second, Janie thought he was going to kiss it.

Linn might have swooned a little, and Janie struggled to keep from grimacing. Rhett was a good-looking guy, for sure. But one realized as soon as he opened his mouth what a doofus he could be. She had thirty-plus years of history with a front-row seat to Rhett's shenanigans.

"We have mud to move. And I'm sure you've...got your own job too." *Now move along, please.*

"I guess I do," Rhett agreed, even though he'd glued his gaze on Linn like a bird of prey spotting a meal scurrying through the grass.

"Thank you for the shovel, Dr. Farr," Linn said. Janie wanted to take her by the shoulders and shake that quiver out of her voice.

Still, Rhett didn't move.

"Nice to see you, Rhett. Bye."

Linn caught on to Janie's dismissal. She cast one last smile over her shoulder for Rhett's benefit before disappearing back into the kitchen. For someone who seemed guarded earlier, Linn didn't put up any walls around handsome doctors.

Someone passed by the picture window outside. Seconds later, Mark easily took up the door frame when he peered inside. Janie stopped shoveling again. Her breath caught. Mark eyed Rhett keeping Janie company, and an almost imperceptible frown tugged at the corners of his mouth. Then he was gone again.

Of course Rhett caught everything. A one-sided smile appeared when he looked back at her.

"Maybe it's not over after all," he said.

Janie pressed her lips together and dug into the mud layer again.

"It's over, Rhett. Just like this conversation."

Chapter Seven

Mark swiped the bandana across his forehead that he'd tucked into his front pocket. Stinging sweat clouded his vision as the afternoon had grown increasingly hot and muggy. The number of volunteers helping in and around the restaurant had thinned as time wore on, and the majority now huddled around the five-gallon water coolers underneath the shade tree near the gazebo, refilling plastic water bottles and thermoses more than they worked.

Janie continued inside the restaurant, making an appearance only once to unload the wheelbarrow full of silt and other debris she'd shoveled, until she realized he was there. Someone else emptied the wheelbarrow after that.

The stench of river water still hung in the air, and the humidity didn't help. It would only get worse as June turned into July. But the worst month in Mark's opinion, when you could practically grab a fistful of air and wring it out like a wet rag, was August. Oh, for a high-country summer again. He missed the mountains of Wyoming and Colorado, two of his favorite states from his travel writing gig. One of his first purchases when he'd arrived back in town and settled into the studio apartment again—a dehumidifier. He'd had it humming along already these last few weeks with all the moisture in the air.

A whistle sounded somewhere close by. Mona Jarvis was back to standing on the gazebo steps.

"We're going to wrap up for today, people. Thank you so much for helping," she said, her voice a little raspy from overuse. Mona was a talker.

"We'll be firing up the grills shortly for the hot dogs," she continued. "There will also be barbecue, chips, and drinks. So, go home, get cleaned up, then come back for a meal at five o'clock so the Hicklebournes can show you their appreciation."

Mark walked the last booth seat over to the flatbed, lifted it onto the platform, and let the two teenagers standing on top of the trailer take over. He pulled out the rag again to mop his brow. A shower sounded like heaven right about now.

The already-sparse crowd broke up in no time. He didn't bother looking for Janie again because no doubt she'd already planned her escape so she wouldn't have to see him again. Mark climbed the wooden stairs at the back of the restaurant and unlocked the door to his apartment and stepped inside.

A thin film of plaster dust on the floor and a few bits from the ceiling above his head greeted him inside the room again. Stewing, he grabbed the broom from the skinny closet in the galley kitchen and swept it into a small pile before scooping the debris into a dustpan.

Mark looked up at the ceiling. An old water spot up there had loosened the plaster enough that it'd started flaking off. A spider web of cracks fanned out from the spot, one snaking all the way across the room to the front windows. Not an alarmist by nature, Mark didn't think anything of it until the crack moved from the ceiling and continued down the wall toward the floor sometime over the last week. He'd been hunkered over his cereal bowl at the counter when he glanced across the room and noticed the crack. It zigzagged down the wall like the meandering western border of Illinois. Thomas Hicklebourne got a call that morning, *pronto*.

And now, even though Thomas and his general contractor friend assured Mark there was nothing to worry about, Mark wasn't so sure. At the very least, Thomas could further discount his rent being that the sky, *er ceiling*, was falling again.

He knew just where to find Thomas.

After a quick shower, Mark took the stairs down to the ground level again and walked into the back door of the restaurant, heading straight to the restaurant's office through the kitchen. There he found Thomas and his teenaged son lifting a metal file cabinet onto a red dolly.

"Thomas, we have a problem."

Tall and rail thin, Thomas's lack of visible muscle mass belied his strength. Mark had seen him in action a short while ago, lifting one side of the commercial oven across the sidewalk to the backend of a truck without breaking a sweat.

"What is it?" Thomas asked, easing the dolly out the office door. He was an amicable guy unless someone crossed him on a hot day. Today had been as steamy as a Grecian sauna. Mark guessed today was not a Thomas the Friendly day.

"That ceiling is shedding again. Something needs to be done, or I'm going to wake up one morning covered in plaster chunks."

"We've kind of got our hands full with, you know"—he

took an exaggerated look around—"the river coming through our restaurant."

"I get it. But I'm paying—"

"Yesyesyes. I hear you." He rested his arms on the top of the cabinet and nodded to his son. "Can you stick your head outside and see if Charles is still lurking around?"

His son let go of the dolly and disappeared around the corner in search of the contractor who'd inspected the cracked ceiling weeks ago.

"Charles assured us it was structurally sound. As soon as we get this cleaned up, I'll have him tear down the ceiling and replace it with drywall."

"I'm not sure it can wait that long, Thomas."

"It'll have to. I need Charles down here so I can get up and running again."

Mark wasn't getting anywhere with the guy. To top it off, his son returned, saying Charles was nowhere in sight.

A few diehards were still at work outside when Mark left the building. He paused mid-step. One of them was Janie. Her back to him, she carried an armload of shovels to a pickup truck, struggling to dump them over the side into the bed.

"Give me a hand with these, will ya?" she shouted at no one in particular, though two young guys scrambled her way to help.

Mark was closer.

"I can help." He waved away the two guys.

She didn't hear him amid the voices around them giving directions, the myriad of equipment still being moved to make way for the meal. This was the perfect chance to ask if she was sticking around to eat. Surely, the smell of barbecue and grilled meat hanging in the air would dull her dislike for him and she'd agree to sit down to talk.

Mark came up behind her and reached around for a few shovels to take off her hands. She yelped in surprise, making her armload clatter to the ground. Janie jumped backward to avoid a shovel landing on her feet, bumping into his chest in the process.

Janie whirled around. She looked ready to attack.

He put his arms up. "I didn't mean to startle you."

"But you did," she said, wide-eyed.

"Sorry, but it looked like you needed help."

She pushed damp strands of hair away from her neck where they'd escaped her ponytail.

"I had everything under control, Mark."

He could argue that point, but it was moot. Janie would fight him to the death on that, being a stubbornly independent sort.

They collected the shovels without another word and threw them all into the pickup. He was about to apologize again when her brother-in-law, Jordan Lorch, hopped out of the cab with his phone at his ear. His eyes darted to Janie, which made her freeze.

"What is it?" she asked with a note of panic in her tone.

Jordan nodded, still listening to whomever was on the other end.

"Janie's here. I'll tell her." He paused, nodding to whatever was said. "Give her my love." Then he tucked his phone in his back pocket.

"Jordan. Tell me."

"Your mom is in the ER. There was a complication with her PICC line."

Mark caught her look of fear when she locked eyes with him.

Jordan touched her arm. "Listen, Janie. I'd offer to drive, but I don't trust this load to not topple off. It needs to be secured first." He nodded to the trailer hitched to his truck. "You should probably get there sooner rather than later."

She peeled off her gloves and dug her keys from her pocket. "That's all right. My car's parked by the cafe."

Mark stepped forward, his hand out for her keys. "I can drive."

Janie looked like she was about to protest even as she willingly gave them up.

She nodded. "Let's go."

Chapter Eight

Mark's offer to take her to the hospital set her senses into overdrive and put her at ease at the same time. It was the familiar feeling she remembered from when they were together—the intense attraction coupled with his comforting presence. Mark was steady, an anchor. His quiet strength was incredibly grounding to her craziness. She felt that now as she followed him to her car, almost like she could reach out and touch it. And it was so like Mark to show up at the exact moment she needed help, swooping in to her rescue.

"What does Sonya—your mom—have a PICC line for?" he asked after they were on the highway headed toward Davenport.

"She cut her leg last month." Her voice cracked, so she cleared it. "Nothing major. It would have healed nicely if she wasn't knee deep in flood waters a few days later, helping a friend."

He winced when she looked at him. "That's not good. So, she's been doing okay until now?"

She shrugged. "I suppose so. You know her. She'd be on her last breath insisting she was fine."

Mark chuckled. "You're a little like her, you know."

She swallowed. There it was again, the feeling that no time had passed at all. That Mark commenting about the similarities between her and her mother was just casual conversation between lovers.

"How so?"

"Resilient. Unflappable."

Had he only seen her in the weeks after she left Port Chance for Minnesota, Mark wouldn't use the word "unflappable." If it hadn't been for her family supporting the move and sticking around until Janie was settled in, she would have filled Lake Superior twice over with tears. Resilient, maybe. She'd come through their separation after a few months. But unflappable? About as unflappable as Monte when his griddle died before the long Thanksgiving weekend years ago during Port Chance's HollyDaze festival. She'd been front row and center for that meltdown.

When she didn't respond, he turned the radio on but kept the volume low.

"So, you came back for her. Your mother," he said.

"I did." Did he expect another reason?

He glanced at her. "How long are you in town for?"

She didn't want to say indefinitely. "I'm not sure."

Mark's chest rose and fell with a deep breath. A familiar country song came on the radio, and he tapped his finger against the steering wheel to the rhythm. But the silent pause was loaded with unspoken questions.

"Listen, Janie. I know this is probably the wrong time—"

"It is, so please don't."

He nodded, keeping his eyes on the road. "Fair enough," he said, though his jaw ticked.

The rest of the drive to the hospital was a quiet one. Mark dropped her off at the emergency room entrance, letting her know he'd be in as soon as he found a parking spot.

Inside, the receptionist buzzed her in through the security doors and gave her the room number. She spotted her sister, Rose, outside the curtained room on her phone. When she saw Janie, Rose tucked her phone away and held out her hand for Janie.

"I think she'll be okay," Rose said. "I came over this afternoon to visit. Mom was outside planting flowers. She kept itching the spot around her port."

"And?" Janie peeked through the gap in the curtain. A nurse blocked her view of Sonya who still wore her green gardening loafers with the daisy design.

"And they think she got into something like poison ivy or sumac. They're giving her an antihistamine." Rose's phone rang again, but she silenced it.

"Jordan had me worried."

Rose rubbed the sides of her face. "That was probably my fault. At that point we didn't have any answers. I'm glad you came, though. Did you drive yourself?"

"I didn't. Mark brought me." She reached for the curtain to slip into her mother's room, but Rose had her by the arm.

"Mark *Christie*?" Rose wore a half-smile like it was some kind of joke.

"Do we know any other Marks?"

"Don't be coy with me. Are you two...talking?" Her sister looked positively rabid with curiosity.

"Yes, we talked."

Rose rolled her eyes. "No, I mean *talked*."

"I don't know what you're implying, but if I had to guess, it's something completely off-base."

Janie reclaimed her arm on her way into the room to see Sonya.

Her mother sat on the edge of the bed with her arm propped onto the metal table before her. A nurse wearing a blue smock covered with illustrated birds held Sonya's arm in one hand and swabbed ointment on the red, raised skin with her other hand. Sonya gritted her teeth while she watched.

"Didn't you get your fill of doctor's offices the other day?" Janie propped herself up against the wall, too anxious to sit at the moment.

"Oh, you know me. I'm always looking for a little excitement," Sonya joked. "The good news is I get to go home. Your father and sister thought I'd be spending the night in the hospital."

"Where is Dad?"

"He's with someone from the billing department, filling out paperwork for insurance," Sonya said.

The nurse glanced at her. "We think *he's* had enough of doctor's offices."

"Where were you working that this happened?" It surprised Janie she'd avoided a rash with as much weeding as she'd done around the property since coming home.

"Along the deck by the creek. That area hasn't been touched in years."

"I'm sure Dad will be torching it now."

The three of them chatted while the nurse finished treating Sonya's rash. Rose joined them a few minutes later after she'd updated the rest of the family.

"Kit and Sadie asked if they should come, but I told them to stay put," Rose said. "They send their love. I'm sure they'll be waiting for us at the house when we get home."

"It's just a rash," Sonya said.

"I'm sure they were as worried as I was when Jordan... *Oh*!" She slapped a hand against her forehead. "Mark's been waiting in the lobby all this time."

Rose and Sonya exchanged knowing looks before Rose dangled Janie's keys in front of her face.

"Are these yours?" Rose asked with an impish grin.

Janie snatched them from her. "You went out there looking for him, didn't you?"

"I happened to be at the vending machine in the lobby, and he was sitting right there," Rose said with a casual air. "We talked."

"You're evil."

"No, just nosy."

"Did he leave?"

Rose chuckled. "He said a friend was coming for him, so he handed over your keys."

Janie groaned. "Now I feel horrible."

"You shouldn't. He understands."

She narrowed her eyes at Rose. "What else did you talk about?"

Rose answered her with a smile before mimicking zipping her lips.

"I'll never tell."

Chapter Nine

I t was like three days had passed instead of three years.

Mark stabbed at his salad, listening to the hum inside the Daisy Gap Cafe while his thoughts raced, replaying the ride to the hospital for the hundredth time in his mind.

Hoping Janie was working the lunch shift today, he purposely showed up at one o'clock on the tail end of the rush. Maybe their ride together broke the ice and she'd slide into his booth like old times and talk his ear off while she filled salt and pepper shakers.

But when he'd come through the front door, Monte spotted him from behind the griddle and gave him a slow, sad shake of his head.

The cafe was half filled. Plates covered in utensils and napkins rested on the ends of tables, waiting to be cleared. Billie's slow pace confirmed the lunch rush was over.

After Billie took his order a few minutes later, Monte personally delivered Mark's grilled cheese and Cobb salad when it was ready.

"How's my friend today?" Monte sat down. He leaned forward and linked his fingers together on the tabletop.

"As good as to be expected considering you lied to me."

Monte pointed to himself with both thumbs, giving Mark a look of exaggerated surprise.

"Yes, you. How come you didn't tell me she'd be at the cafe before we saw each other that first time?"

"Who?" Monte was a terrible liar.

"Don't play dumb. You know exactly who I mean."

Monte did his characteristic face rub when confronted, as if the weight of the world was in his answer and staying silent would spare everyone the misery of knowledge.

"I didn't think it was important. I mean, you two are done. Finished. *Kaput*." Monte winced. "Sorry, man."

"Thanks for the reminder."

"Hey, I tried. What do you think I was trying to do by not telling you? Catch you both by surprise, that's what."

Mark huffed. "How was that supposed to help?"

"When your guard's down, the true feelings come out."

Mark squinted. "That doesn't sound like something you'd come up with."

Monte groaned. "Fine. It was Camilla's idea."

"I was going to say maybe you should stick to cooking."

"It was all with good intentions. I hated when you two called it quits. You guys were like scrambled eggs and bacon."

He was quickly losing his taste for lunch. Monte's inability to mince words was a gut punch.

Monte got up again. "That woman is ice, man. Sorry."

Mark waved him off. "No need to be sorry."

"By the way, where are you taking me for my bachelor party?"

"Aren't we too old for bachelor parties?"

Monte looked hurt. "Speak for yourself."

"I'm joking. It's a surprise, but be sure to wear your Guillen jersey."

Monte's eyes bugged out. "Seriously, man? We're going to a game?"

Mark laughed. "I said it's a surprise. Now you'd better get back to work. I may be footing the bill for the bachelor party, but I heard you're covering the wedding. I'm sure there are bills to pay."

His friend clutched at his chest with both hands. "No joke. I told her no more family. I don't even know half the people on the guest list."

"You could have eloped."

"I suggested it. Almost lost my burger-flipping arm." He pretended to cut his arm off at the shoulder.

Once Monte headed back to the kitchen, Mark poked at his salad again while the Janie-sized hole in his chest grew a little wider. Even if landing in Port Chance again was intentional, earning Janie's trust again wasn't at the top of his agenda. Okay, that was a lie. A second chance with her *was* wishful thinking, but there were other reasons for returning. He'd built a connection to the community, first as a newspaper advertising rep, then when he moved to town permanently. He'd missed that while on the road. Now he was ready to settle down. He hoped to move on from the perpetual renter's status.

His thoughts turned to Adelia Goodwin again. Seeing her on the bike path the other day got him thinking about the storage unit she'd allowed him to use for his mother's furnishings years ago. He'd locked away Muriel Christie's treasures, not ready for the reminder that she was no longer alive. The idea that her antiques, the objects she and Mark painstakingly sought out during their Saturdays together, might be sold and parsed out to strangers was unacceptable. But what would a twenty-something guy living in a college apartment have done with a Hepplewhite sideboard or an emerald, velvet Chesterfield loveseat? So Adelia had offered to keep two rooms' worth of furniture and other belongings in her personal storage unit in downtown Davenport indefinitely. Now it was time to make a change.

Admittedly, connections were hard for him. He had very little to show for his forty-two years in terms of relationships. His mother was dead. He'd never known his biological father. His stepfather had no interest in maintaining a relationship once Mark's mother passed. Janie had been the longest-term relationship he'd ever had, but that was history too. Port Chance had given him a small opportunity to find his place in the world. He'd left once—for the job, he liked to tell himself. But had he also been running away from commitment? In the end, it didn't matter. Janie had beat him to the punch, leaving for a fresh start in Minnesota. And now that he'd come to terms with their breakup, Port Chance was where he wanted to be, whether Janie was here or not.

"I didn't get a chance to thank you for the other day."

His fork clattered against his plate in surprise. Janie was here after all.

"I was on my break," Janie said, as if answering his unspoken question.

He nodded, dumbstruck by her presence. Her hair was piled high on her head with a few loose tendrils brushing her shoulders. So used to seeing her with shorter hair when they'd been together, its length transfixed him. The bun accentuated the upward slant of her eyes, but he'd love to see it down.

"Anyway, I appreciate the ride. And I'm sorry for forgetting you were waiting for me," she said.

He set his fork down. "How is your mother?"

"Better. The infection turned out to be a reaction to something she got into in the yard."

"That's good news. I'm glad it wasn't anything to do with her ongoing problems."

Janie nodded.

He tried to think of something to carry on the conversation, but his thoughts spun in frustrating circles.

"It looks like Billie's got you taken care of," she said finally.

"She does."

She eyed his plate, biting her lip like something else was on the tip of her tongue, but ultimately decided against bringing it up.

The pulse beating in his neck quickened with each second that she stood there. He still wanted a few uninterrupted minutes with her without the distraction of a community-wide cleanup, a busy cafe, or an emergency room visit. Janie had brushed him off each time he tried. Maybe she sensed he wanted to talk about where they stood. Maybe she'd decided there was nothing more to discuss.

"See you," she said.

He deflated. There were no "maybes." Janie already knew where he belonged. She'd already decided three years ago.

He was history.

Chapter Ten

I f she ever decided she needed another do-over in life, Janie wouldn't run off again to another state like her Minnesota sojourn.

Granted, she loved the three years she'd spent in Hendricks. Her parents' good friends tipped her off about the little town on Lake Superior where they'd bought a retirement home. It'd been a spontaneous move but she hadn't been thinking rationally after breaking up with Mark. In the end, though, moving to Hendricks had been just what she needed—a fresh start. The job at Fernando's where her boss basically let her decide her own work schedule had been ideal. The side job she'd taken as a nanny because she hated having so much down time without a social life left her with soul-satisfying gratitude too. Then her friendship with Cora Martin blossomed from Janie's weekly visits to the library, and her librarian friend talked her into joining the monthly book club. Her work life kept her busy enough, and she'd filled in the empty spaces with a satisfactory bit of fun too.

But if she ever decided to overhaul her life again, she'd run away closer to home. Namely, Rose's home, or rather the one her sister married into. Driving up the gravel lane later that day toward Apple Hill Orchard was a scene taken right from a spring-inspired calendar. The apple trees in full bloom looked as heavenly as Janie imagined they'd smell if she rolled her window down. A new barn quilt hung above the door of the main red barn. The hulking building wore a fresh coat of cardinal-red paint and was topped with a recently replaced gray metal roof too. White fencing ran the length of the driveway on either side and disappeared over a rolling hill which hid the river from view to the north. That same hill kept the river at bay last month, and Rose said she'd be thanking the heavens daily for that for the rest of her life. A newer building Rose opened as a venue for wedding receptions and corporate retreats just last month would host Monte and Camilla's wedding reception in a few weeks—the first event to take place amid its rustic elegance.

Janie parked her car near the orchard's shop, certain she'd find her sister inside since it was her favorite place on the farm. She hadn't even set one foot outside the car when Rose's oldest boy, Travis, ran across the yard to greet her.

"Hey, Auntie Janie! Mom's inside," he said, his voice crackling an octave lower. *Twelve years old already*, Janie thought. *Where has the time gone?*

He followed her inside the store, regaling her with a story about the oldest of their barn cats cornering a bull snake earlier that morning. Janie made Travis laugh by covering her ears and singing to drown him out.

Rose looked up from the front counter where she stood pricing apples made of blown glass. She carefully set the one in her hand on the shelf behind her.

"What's with the commotion? You're going to shatter these to pieces with all that noise," she said with a chuckle.

Janie ruffled Travis's hair. "Your kid is harassing me. You know how I get with talk about snakes."

Rose gave her son a good-natured shake of her head. "Go tell your dad to turn off the Crockpot. I'll be there in fifteen minutes."

Travis snuck a wrapped caramel from the candy bin next to the counter and winked at his mother before he took off again out the door.

Janie giggled. "That kid. If I ever get lucky enough to have any, I want a duplicate of him." She glanced behind her through the window as Travis scrambled across the yard toward the house, all knees and elbows. "He's equal parts sweet and ornery."

Rose's brows lifted. "These days I only see the ornery part."

Janie leaned against the counter and picked up one of the glass apples. When she looked up to ask Rose the price, Janie spotted Linn, the woman who'd worked near her at the gazebo. Janie waved when Linn spotted her, and Linn gave her a hearty wave back.

She turned over the apple in her hand. The lights above caught the swirls of red and fuchsia on the surface. A glass stem curled from the top with a single, delicate lime-green leaf.

"These are so pretty." She handed it over to Rose who tied a string on the stem with a price tag attached.

"Rory is such an amazing artist. Her new pieces always top what she's done the season before. Have you seen her pumpkins?"

Janie shook her head, not wanting to think about glass

pumpkins at the moment. There were more pressing matters to attend to before she headed back home.

"I came by to drop off those two side tables I've been working on. That, and to get a quick peek at the flowers for Monte and Camilla's wedding."

Rose placed another priced apple on the shelf and turned back with a puzzled look on her face.

"Why the concern about the flowers? Did Monte put you up to that?"

"Yes. Why?"

"Because Camilla asked me to make the arrangements." Rose shrugged.

"He only asked if I'd move the wedding day flowers from the wedding to the reception. But I thought I'd surprise them and make up some little arrangements for the tables Friday night for the rehearsal dinner."

Rose nodded, her attention now occupied with cleaning up the counter. Behind her, across the shop, the bakery area went dark. Linn Miranelli came out from behind the counter wearing a white apron. She smiled when she noticed Janie and handed each of them a frosted, apple-shaped sugar cookie.

"It's nice to see you again, Janie," Linn said.

Rose looked up. "So, you two have already met."

Linn nodded. "At the Yellow Pier when we were helping with the cleanup."

"Speaking of which, is another one planned?" Rose asked. "Travis had a ball game that day and Jordan was already volunteering there."

"I believe in two weeks." Janie checked the time on her phone. "Should we get those tables in here? I've got to get back to the house."

Rose and Linn followed her outside.

Janie opened the hatch of her car to lift one side table out, then the other. She'd repurposed some of the barn wood Jordan had salvaged for her when he took down one of the dilapidated buildings on the property. It was solid hardwood with a nice grain. She'd assembled them after searching for examples online. Then she'd sanded, stained, and sealed the pieces in her spare time, enjoying the solitude of working in her father's woodshop after dinner, listening to the sound of the mourning doves and crickets as the sun dipped behind the house.

"These are beautiful," Linn said, running a hand across the top. "Where'd you learn how to do this?"

Janie shrugged. "Our dad is a contractor. I guess I was more interested in power tools than dolls growing up. And he's a patient man."

Rose huffed, grinning. "Between you and Kit, I'm surprised he survived your childhood." She and Linn each took an end and carried them from the car back into the shop. Janie shut the hatch then picked up the other table to bring inside.

"What do you think we should price these at?" Rose asked.

"Beats me." Janie did have a figure in mind but waited for Rose to go first. Whatever Rose decided, Janie's portion would supplement what she made at the diner. Living in the guest house wasn't permanent. Eventually, she needed her own place.

"I'm going to look at your garden for cuttings. Let me know what you decide." Janie backed toward the door. "I've got to get going since dinner's on me tonight."

Rose's look of surprise made Janie laugh. She threw her arms out. "What?"

"You've changed," Rose said. "Now you cook?"

"I'm still the same sister you know and love. 'Cooking' means I'm buying pizza."

Janie cleared the plates from the table, stacking them next to the dishwasher after dinner that night. She glanced through the window as she ran the sink faucet. Outside, the last of the sun's glow barely registered on the horizon. The first stars blinked in the sky.

Sonya and Aaron were still at the dining room table. Behind Janie, the crack of her dad shuffling cards made her smile. Blackjack or Crazy Eights after dinner had long been the tradition for as long as Janie could remember. The kids would scatter, leaving her parents to enjoy each other's company while rehashing their day and talking about the week ahead. When Mimi was alive, she'd join in for a few hands until she too would retreat to the living room or outside on the porch in good weather. Mimi had known the value of alone time for a husband and wife. She'd lost her own husband way too early in life.

"Why don't you play with us, honey?"

Janie froze while rinsing a plate. "Seriously?" She whirled around to check for evidence that Sonya was joking.

"Of course."

"This is the first time you've ever opened up your after-dinner games to one of us. What gives?"

Sonya hitched a shoulder. Under the overhead light, her hair shone, halo-like. "Nothing. Just wondered if you wanted in."

Janie loaded the last two plates into the dishwasher before she joined them. Aaron dealt them each eight cards. It had been so long since Janie played, she realized she needed a quick refresher after scooping up her cards and drawing a blank on the first move.

While Aaron explained the rules, Sonya refilled their glasses with sweet tea. After catching Sonya's eye for the fifth time in less than a minute, Janie knew Sonya's motive for asking if she wanted to play wasn't because she thought Janie was bored.

"I can hear your thoughts, Mom. What is it?"

Sonya kept her eyes on the cards in her hand. "It's nothing."

"Anytime you say 'it's nothing,' it's *always* something."

"Just tell her, Sonya. She'll find out anyway."

Janie dropped her cards and sighed. "Spill it, please."

"Mark came by today," Sonya said. "He wanted to see how I was doing."

"That's nice." Her pulse rushed with an irregular rhythm at the mention of his name before she took a deep breath.

"I thought you should know in case you heard from someone else and thought I might be keeping it from you on purpose," Sonya said. Her gaze lingered on Janie.

Janie drew a card. "I appreciate it." She didn't have to look up to know her parents exchanged glances.

"Do you have plans to get together now that he's back too?" Sonya asked.

"No. Why would I?" She kept her eyes on her cards.

"Because you were together three years. Because you cared deeply for each other."

"So deeply that he chose a job over me."

"Janie, honey. Don't you think you've held this grudge long enough? It's clear he's trying to make things right."

"Why is making Mark feel better more important than what I'm going through?"

"What are you going through, exactly?"

She'd played right into Sonya's hands. All along she'd tried to pretend she was okay with her and Mark's breakup. It'd been easy living more than five hundred miles away. She didn't live under a microscope there. Now with Mark arriving back in town around the same time she'd returned, people were talking. What she didn't count on was being scrutinized by her own family.

"I'm not going through anything. But we haven't spoken in three years, Mom." She set her cards down now that it was impossible to talk and concentrate on the game at the same time. "It's been over for some time now. And suddenly, now that we're both back in Port Chance, we're supposed to pick up where we left off? No, thank you."

"You two were so good together. And with him settling back in town, it has a better chance of working out this time."

"But you're forgetting one little detail. He left."

"You left first," Aaron said, so quietly Janie barely caught the words. He usually was a silent bystander to the heavier conversations.

She did leave first. From all outward appearances, it was Janie who called it quits. But she couldn't stay behind in a place that was flooded with memories. It would have destroyed her. Leaving Port Chance was a self-defense move, but no one needed to know that.

"What's to say he won't leave again?" Janie stood. Heat flooded her face. She couldn't talk about Mark. Not to her parents, not to anyone. Her throat felt like it was closing up. "I've moved on from this a long time ago."

"If you think he's like that other one—"

Janie put her hand up before Sonya could finish. "Like Jason? No."

Aaron got up from the table too, giving Sonya a cross look. "That was ages ago, Sonya. Why'd you have to bring that up?"

"Because maybe it explains why she hasn't had a meaningful relationship that *lasts*." Sonya looked back at Janie. Her expression softened.

"Sit down, please," Sonya said. "I didn't mean to upset you."

"I don't want to discuss Mark." Janie didn't like her clipped tone, but they'd put her on the defensive. "Or Jason."

"We won't bring it up again." Sonya reached across the table to rub her arm. "We're just thankful you're here now."

"I'm happy to be back. Really, I am. But these constant hints from people that they'd like to see us patch things up are nerve-racking."

Sonya tilted her head. "I'm sorry. Who else has brought it up?"

"Kit. Rhett Farr. Monte hasn't said anything but that in itself caused the biggest problem of all." Aaron and Sonya gave her a quizzical look, but she waved them off. "Never mind."

"From now on, this house will be a Mark-free zone," Sonya said as she threw down a card.

"Thank you." Janie took another breath to clear the tension in her chest. Her pounding heart started to slow, but she couldn't clear her thoughts.

As they finished two more rounds of cards, Janie didn't believe that talk of Mark and her was finished—in this house or in Port Chance for that matter.

But what bothered Janie most, despite her denials both

aloud and to herself, was the idea that she and Mark would always be a couple in her heart of hearts.

Chapter Eleven

The next morning, Janie drifted out of sleep on the tail of a dream—one she couldn't quite put into words, but she knew it had been about Mark. It was the kind of dream that would linger in her conscience throughout the day, adding a layer of subtle pleasure to every mundane task. Maybe he'd gently cupped her face in his hands, had brushed her lips with a teasing kiss, nuzzled his cheek against hers and closed his eyes. Whatever the details of the dream, it made her feel as light as air, like she might float through the day if gravity wasn't such an undeniable force.

Still lying in bed, Janie found herself wondering when she'd see Mark again. The low timbre of his voice never failed to thrill her even while she still harbored hard feelings about their breakup. Her mouth went dry thinking about it now.

What are you doing?

Before more dangerous thoughts surfaced, Janie bounded out of bed. The cold wood floor bit the bottoms of her bare feet as she crossed the room, throwing on her cardigan in the process. The only solution to keeping Mark out of her mind was to keep busy. She'd simply outrun her thoughts. There was more work to do on the flower beds, and after lunch, she'd stop by the boutique on Main Street to dress shop for Monte's wedding.

After a quick breakfast, she dressed, grabbed the clippers from the garden shed, and headed for another untamed part of the property. This time, the peony bed where the gum-ball-sized buds would burst open any day was in her crosshairs. They were probably her favorite flower, with lush, palm-sized blooms in fuchsia and others in white with a tinge of pink edging. Fragrant too. The ants loved them. Of course, honeysuckle shoots had taken over here too.

Janie settled onto a folding stool and slipped on her gloves. The morning air was sweet with the scent of cut grass and dew-soaked foliage. She took in the scene beyond the flower bed, finding peace of mind with the sight of clematis climbing the blue garden trellis at the side of the guest cottage. A row of brightly colored birdhouses hung on the side wall of the little house, sparrows flitting in and out of the holes, apparently shopping for the perfect nesting space.

But then her attention turned to the cedar bench with the arch and planter boxes spilling over with pink petunias and sweet potato vines near the rear of the cottage, and what—or whom—she'd struggled to put out of her mind all morning came rushing at her again.

Mark had helped build that bench. Memories of that day were burned into her mind. The scent of freshly cut cedar. Sunlight on his arms as he held pieces of the arch together as she set screws and drilled. How Mark's eyes rested on her while she stood back to admire their handiwork.

We should star in one of those home improvement shows together. We're a pretty good team, she remembered saying.

There was a falter in his smile before he nodded. *That we are*, he'd answered. But the look he'd given her put her senses on high alert.

Shortly after he'd emptied bags of soil into the planters, they'd sat down to test the bench's strength. Then he'd told her about the writing opportunity that would take him away from her. Mark wanted to take it; it was the job of a lifetime. Lucrative. Exciting. A challenge. He'd also asked if she'd come with him.

As she snipped and pulled weeds, more images played in her mind like a movie trailer. How the excitement had lit Mark's face. Them shopping for a pickup camper the next week to make living on the road cheaper. The heated disagreements between them after she told Mark she didn't want to go after all.

Mark hadn't understood her decision.

At first, she didn't either. She'd loved him. Shouldn't she jump at the chance for an adventure with the man she loved, just the two of them? But then it dawned on her. What she'd expected after dating three years was a tangible promise of their future together, not an invitation to live out of a camper. She'd wanted a ring.

She'd agonized over her feelings. She was both proud of Mark and truly happy his dream of making a living as a writer had come true. But her own needs overshadowed everything. Uprooting her life to follow him seemed premature at best. She'd tried to make him see her point of view without asking for a commitment outright. Sure, they'd talked about marriage. *Someday.* But they never moved beyond the casual talk.

Janie sat back on the stool and dropped the clippers into the flower bed. Honeysuckle blossoms clung to the ends of her hair. She plucked them out, scowling.

Had her mother hit on something when she mentioned Jason? It was so long ago. They'd barely been out of high school when they got engaged. And then even before a date was set, Jason found someone else.

Engagement called off. Ring returned. Heart broken.

Janie had never experienced the sting of rejection on such a scale, and at the time, she promised herself she'd never put herself in that position again. But her relationship with Mark had been different. Or was it?

Janie tossed the blossoms into the grass and ground them with her heel. Despite the mellow mood she'd woken up with that morning, she was back to stewing.

What would it take to get over Mark Christie once and for all?

After doing battle with the honeysuckle all morning, Janie pulled into one of the parallel parking spots in front of Threads Up!, a boutique not much bigger than a walk-in closet, later that day. The shop sat on the steepest slope of Main Street, two storefronts up from the Yellow Pier restaurant, but the flood waters stopped well before reaching the building. The front door was propped open with a green ladder-back chair. A clay pot filled with red geraniums rested on the seat for a cheery welcome. An "open" sign hung from a hook beside the nine-pane window. It was as charming inside as was its owner, Becky.

Still a little dazed from the dream, Janie stopped short over the threshold inside.

She blinked.

Mark stood in front of the three-panel mirror with his arms out while Becky Chu stretched a tape measure from his armpit to his wrist. His gaze met hers when they locked eyes in the mirror.

"Janie, hi! Were your ears burning? We were just talking about you. I wondered when I'd see you here," Becky said, taking her eyes off Mark's arm long enough to give Janie a quick smile. In the mirror, Mark's face turned a shade similar to Becky's rose-colored dress.

"I see you're busy. I can come back." Janie backed toward the door when Becky protested.

"Nonsense. Mark and I are almost finished," she said. "Some really cute dresses came in. I've put two aside for you." She winked. "I think they're just what you're looking for."

Janie shook her head. "I don't want you to rush what you're doing. I've got an errand to run." She thumbed over her shoulder, backing toward the threshold.

Becky pointed with the tape measure. "Watch your st—"

Too late. Janie's heel caught the raised portion of the threshold, and she stumbled backward, bumping the chair and upending the geranium pot. It splintered onto the pavement next to her with a dull *thud*.

Mark was beside her in an instant.

"Are you all right?" he and Becky asked simultaneously.

"I'm fine, thank you," she said, feeling foolish as she scooped handfuls of soil over the visible bare roots of the plant. Luckily, her bottom took the brunt of the fall. The only thing bruised was her ego.

"Don't worry about the plant," said Becky. "I have another

pot in the storeroom." She disappeared into the shop and returned with a garbage can and a broom.

"It's dangerous trying to avoid me all the time" he said, holding her arm with one hand and encircling her back with the other. "Maybe you should change tactics."

"I'm fine, thank you," she said curtly as her entire body hummed with the effect of his touch. Janie straightened herself, tugging at the straps of her sundress which had gone slightly askew. She was as graceful as a water buffalo in his presence. Why did he happen to be everywhere she was in Port Chance?

Becky swept up the mess of pottery shards and plucked the homeless geranium off the sidewalk and into the shop.

Mark walked Janie back inside.

"You're sure you're okay?" His hand still rested on her back. The sensation made her think back to a time when she loved his touch. Now it was irritating because it just made it hard for her to breathe.

Janie stepped away and faced him. *Safely out of reach.*

"I'm positive." Her gaze met his at the same second. All she could think about was the dream. The skin on her forearms tingled. Thankfully, Becky reentered the room at that moment.

"Mark, I think we're finished with the measurements. I'll give you a call when the suit comes in."

He nodded. "Sounds good," he said, moving toward the door. But then he paused, his gaze focused on Janie again. "See you around."

Janie stood frozen as he left the shop, watching him go.

Behind her, Becky pushed clothes to either side of the rolling rack beside the counter. "It sounds like you both will be at Monte and Camilla's wedding. I bet that new venue at the orchard will be such a beautiful backdrop for a reception."

A newcomer to Port Chance, Becky wasn't privy to her backstory with Mark. Janie welcomed the chance to talk with someone who wouldn't give her the third degree about her and Mark getting back together.

"Rose and Jordan have put their hearts and souls into that building. I can't wait to see it filled with people."

"Camilla asked me to do the alterations on her wedding dress. Talk about pressure." Becky held up one of the dresses she'd recommended for Janie. It was petal pink with cap sleeves and a flouncy chiffon skirt. She loved the lace overlay and the pink seed pearls outlining the scoop neckline. "This one will look beautiful with your skin tone."

Janie carried the dress into the dressing room, continuing the conversation through the curtain.

"Monte mentioned Camilla's dress is vintage?"

Beyond the curtain, Becky unzipped the other dress she had waiting. "Her mother's. Stunning. You have to see the embroidered bodice."

Janie opened the curtain to let Becky fasten the one pearl closure at the back of her neck. When Becky got a look at Janie in the dress, she whistled.

"That dress was *made* for you," she crowed. "Your someone special is going to be all eyes on you at the wedding."

"There's no one special."

"Oh, then you'll certainly have one by the end of the night wearing that!"

Janie laughed and pointed at the other dress Becky had flung over her arm. "Then maybe I should try on that one."

With Mark gone, she relaxed and fell into the easy conversation with Becky as she tried on the other dress and a slew of tops Becky kept feeding her through the curtain. Becky was right;

she loved both dresses. Now to decide which one to wear to the wedding.

In the distance, the rumble of a train on the outskirts of town interrupted their conversation. Janie lifted the hangers with shirts from the hook in her dressing room and pushed back the curtain. Any second, the whistle would blow when it neared the Route 67 crossing; she knew this from thirty years of living near the tracks. Normally the sound blended into the background like the sound of a mower or the hum of traffic. But something was off. The whistle didn't come seconds later after all. And the floor boards under her feet started to vibrate. That never happened.

Alarmed, she looked up to find Becky staring back at her with the same concerned expression.

"What is that?" Becky asked.

The rumble grew louder, sending a rack of necklaces swinging nearby. Becky gripped the counter.

"What's happening? What is that?" Becky repeated, this time more frantic.

Janie tried to swallow the dreadful feeling filling her throat.

Outside, someone ran past the shop door.

A shout of "Get back!" spurred Janie to hurry outside with Becky close behind her.

Two more people ran past her down the sidewalk. The activity, coupled with a deafening roar, stopped her short as she looked down the block toward the Yellow Pier restaurant.

Or rather what *used to be* the Yellow Pier restaurant.

She choked on a cry.

A cloud of debris and dust billowed upward and outward as the upper story of the building collapsed into the restaurant portion with the loudest *boom* yet.

Janie's knees would have buckled had she not reached for the man standing next to her. He too was frozen in shock.

Her first thought manifested itself into one word.

"*Mark*!"

Chapter Twelve

He couldn't see.

He couldn't breathe.

And most frightening of all, he couldn't even hear, except for a high-pitched ringing in his head.

Mark lay sprawled out on the ground, one of his kitchen stools—now missing two legs—inches from his face. He scrambled to find his footing amongst chunks of brick, plaster, and splintered wood. All around him hung a dust cloud as if fog had descended over the town. Up ahead, the pitched roof of the gazebo appeared through the haze. But something was wrong.

Horribly wrong.

He shouldn't be able to see the gazebo from where he now stood. Not with the Yellow Pier restaurant between him and Main Street. But...only half of the restaurant still stood. The rest was a jumble of debris. Somewhere in there was his apartment.

He used his shirt sleeve to wipe dust and sweat from his face, hoping to clear his vision. The fabric came away bloody.

His fingers found the sticky spot near his temple, and he wiped that on his shirt too.

Trying to make sense of what happened, Mark stared at the heap of rubble. He'd begun to climb the stairs at the back of his apartment when the ground shook. He'd never experienced an earthquake, but he fully expected the ground to open up and swallow him that instant. Instead, the force of the building imploding blew him off his feet. He'd almost landed on the hood of Tom's truck, but he bounced off of the side panel instead. Now he felt the dull ache in his shoulder where it met the side view mirror.

One thing was important—he was alive.

For the second time in a few minutes, he was taken by surprise.

Someone burst through the haze, running at him, and embraced him around the neck, almost taking him off his feet again.

Her voice sounded distant as if underwater, but he could hear after all.

Janie.

"Mark," she said over and over again. Her arms loosened, but then she was kissing his cheek, his chin, the hollow of his throat.

His arms found their way around Janie's back despite the pain in his shoulder, and he pulled her to him. Janie's muffled sobs against his chest reverberated throughout his body. Her fear was his fear. Her hands rubbing his back, pulling him closer, threading themselves through his hair mirrored his actions too.

He scanned the rubble, not really seeing it, because all he

could think about at that moment was how much he'd missed Janie. Missed *this*.

Janie looked up at him. While her wide, brown eyes searched his, Mark's focus was squarely on the proximity of her lips. Soft, rose petal pink. It didn't take much effort to remember how they felt. Was she thinking the same thing too?

"Janie ..."

Janie pulled away but held him steady by his arms while she looked him up and down.

"Are you hurt? You don't look hurt." But then she zeroed in on the cut near his eye. "Except for that. We should get you looked at. Praise *God*, you're all right."

He was still dazed. Janie studied him with her brows knit together. Her arm around his waist now, Janie steered him in the direction of a pickup truck. She pulled down the tailgate and pointed for him to sit.

"Maybe you're not okay after all," she said.

"Whose truck is this?" He eased himself on the tailgate.

"Doesn't matter." She held his face between her hands while she examined the cut again now that they were at eye level. The urge to kiss her was so strong, he had to look away from her face.

In the distance, sirens wailed. His attention drifted over her shoulder again at the massive pile of brick, lath, and plaster. Somewhere in there was his futon. What few photos he owned from his childhood. His illustrated UK edition of *Moby Dick* and a signed first edition of *The Grapes of Wrath*.

Oh, his laptop too.

"I can't believe you walked away from that." Janie shook her head as her eyes welled up again.

He huffed, touching the wound near his temple again.

"Had you not tripped, giving me the chance to exercise my chivalry, my afternoon would look a whole lot different right now."

She didn't smile. In fact, his joke had the opposite effect. The tears spilled over at once as she threw herself against him again, sobbing into his collar.

His arms went around her.

"I'm okay, Janie. Really." No lie, it'd be perfect sitting here all afternoon, trying to convince her that except for a little blood and a sore shoulder, he was in pretty good shape. Her closeness was the best medicine anyone could offer.

"But you're right," she said, sniffling in his ear. "You could have been inside your apartment if I'd had my way."

"What do you mean?"

She shook her head, dabbing at her eyes.

"Janie." He held her at arm's length. "It worked out for the best."

"I wanted you to leave. I didn't want to be near you."

"Don't think about that. I'm here now."

A crowd had gathered in the street but was quickly dispersed when emergency vehicles arrived. Janie waved at one of the paramedics when they got out of the ambulance, and they hurried across the empty lot toward him and Janie. Once the cut on his face was treated, Janie insisted they look at his shoulder, but he refused further medical attention. More important issues were at hand than a little scratch and some bruises. He was sure rest and ibuprofen would take care of the inevitable soreness.

"It's not just a scratch, Mark," Janie argued, eyeing his now bandaged cut. "It could use a stitch or two."

Behind her, the female paramedic shook her head, agreeing with Mark.

He took Janie's hand. "I appreciate your concern, but it's nothing a bandage won't take care of."

She pursed her lips but otherwise accepted his decision.

It was determined that no one was in the restaurant when the building collapsed after someone said Tom left town earlier that day, and it was quickly confirmed. The poor guy must be devastated. The Yellow Pier was no longer a renovation project. Tom would have to start from scratch, if that was in the future at all.

He and Janie walked up to the cafe, stopping along the way to talk with those who asked if he was okay. Monte noticed them walk into the cafe and greeted him with a hug.

"You scared the salt and pepper out of me, man," Monte said. "Whatever I can get you is on the house."

Mark realized he was still covered in dust. "We should probably get something to go."

Janie noticed too when she gave him a once-over. She looked as dazed as he felt. "How about two hamburger meals to go. Thank you, Monte," she said.

He excused himself to use the restroom. The few diners in the cafe stared at him as he made his way to the back of the restaurant. In the bathroom, he went straight to the mirror and looked at his reflection.

What a sight I am.

His skin was chalky from the dust coating. His hair too. Blood seeped through the bandage already. He ran the faucet and splashed water on his face, then wiped it clean with a towel from the dispenser. An improvement, but not by much.

Janie sat at the counter on one of the round stools when he came out of the bathroom a few minutes later.

"You look better at least," Janie said.

"Until I get a shower and find a change of clothes, I won't feel like it."

"So, there's a plan," she said. "Wanna hear it?"

He smiled. This was the old, take-charge Janie he remembered.

"Do I have a choice?"

Janie ignored him. "Jordan is getting you some clothes from Farm and Fleet as we speak. You'll be staying in the cottage for the time being while we figure out options for the longer term."

"One question. Where will you be if I'm in the cottage?" That cottage was small for one person. They'd be practically on top of each other if they were both under one roof. Not a bad scenario, but he was certain Janie wasn't thinking clearly if that's what she was suggesting.

"I'll move into my old bedroom in the house."

"Janie, I can stay in the house."

"No. You'll need privacy to work, and my mom is already over the moon you'll be staying with them."

"Work? Have you forgotten my laptop is under forty tons of brick down the block."

She frowned. "Yeah, that kind of slipped my mind."

Monte came out of the kitchen with a paper bag.

"I put an extra burger and fries in there, buddy. For a midnight snack." He shrugged.

Mark took the bag. "Are you implying I'm gonna have a sleepless night?"

"If you don't, your nerves are steelier than the look Camilla gives me when I give out free food." Monte put a finger against his lips. "Don't tell."

"We won't," Janie said, hooking an arm around Mark's and pulling him toward the door. Monte waggled his eyebrows at him when Janie turned her back, but Mark warded off the look with a shake of his head.

Outside, Janie paused on the sidewalk outside the diner. Her car was parked along the curb at the corner.

"I didn't mean to be pushy," she said, looking up the street toward her car. "You know, about staying at the cottage. If you have a better idea, I'm fine with it."

"Are you saying you're...uncomfortable with me being there?"

She gave a quick shake of her head. "No. Why would I be?"

What a fool he was. Of course she wouldn't be uncomfortable. Janie had wasted no time making it clear she was long over him. Even after her emotional display at finding him okay, she'd kept him at arm's length. The same couldn't be said about him. His thoughts still lingered on the fact that he'd almost kissed her. To Janie, Mark lived squarely in the friend zone.

He chuckled with a nonchalant air, trying to save a little face. "No reason. It's just guilt getting the best of me for kicking you back to your childhood bedroom."

Janie threw him a wry look. "I think you know me better than that. *You're* not kicking me out of anywhere. I'm *letting* you stay there. Let's go."

It was one trait that attracted him to Janie when they first met—her take-charge, indomitable spirit. Except now it might be working against him.

Chapter Thirteen

Janie edged the bedroom sheers aside just enough so she could peer across the lawn to the cottage. It had been two days since the building collapse. Two days since Mark had moved into the comforts of her cottage. She'd lost count of the number of times she'd looked out her window for any sign of him since yesterday morning. So far, Mark had done a remarkable imitation of a ghost. No one would guess there was anyone in there by looking at it. Curtains were drawn. The door remained closed. His truck sat parked in the same spot he'd left it along the row of hollyhocks on the south side of the cottage.

Sonya and Aaron had served a breakfast fit for royalty yesterday—a comfort meal for Mark because of his traumatic afternoon the day before. He was welcome to stay as long as he wanted, they had insisted more than once. Her parents were still in love with him. Their gushing gave Janie heartburn. It couldn't possibly be the sage-sausage casserole her mother usually reserved for Christmas morning brunch.

What was he doing in there for the past thirty-six hours?

Her phone rang on the nightstand. She sat down on the feather-down quilt to take the call.

"Hello?"

"Janie. Bad news." Rose's ominous tone was proof that she was serious.

"What is it?"

"Tom Hicklebourne called. He wants to bow out of catering Monte's wedding." Rose groaned as if the enormity of what it meant finally dawned on her. "There's too much on his plate right now, but he doesn't know what to do."

"I can't imagine the pressure he's feeling, but still. What did you say?"

Rose sighed. "I asked if he told Monte yet."

"And did he?"

"No."

Janie pressed a hand to her forehead. "You're kidding. The wedding's in three weeks."

"I know. I think he hoped I would break the news since it's our venue."

Monte would be devastated. Where could he find someone to cater the wedding on such short notice?

"I was waiting for this to happen. Frankly, I thought Tom might cancel after the restaurant was flooded," Rose said. "Apparently, a few of his staff are looking for new jobs now that there's no chance of opening any time soon."

"Right. At least he was paying them to help with clean up so he could keep them on staff."

"And now they're gone."

"I'll talk to Tom. Maybe we can work something out." Exactly what that would be, Janie hadn't a clue. And Janie didn't know Tom very well, but Mark did as his tenant. It'd be the perfect excuse to knock on the door and see what Mark was up to. She'd rally Mark to come with her.

"Let me know what you find out," Rose said. "No one can sweet talk better than you. My fingers are crossed for Monte."

After Janie said goodbye to Rose, she slipped on a cardigan and her loafers. With one last peek out the window toward the cottage, she headed downstairs.

* * *

After knocking three times, Janie started to think Mark wasn't in the cottage after all.

Or maybe he was and chose to avoid her on purpose after he saw her coming.

She leaned forward, pressing her ear against the door.

No music. No footsteps. *Silence.*

But as she stepped off the front porch, the door swung open. Mark tugged a sweatshirt over his stomach.

"Sorry. Late shower," he said. He ran a hand through his damp hair, which stood up in haphazard spikes.

But it was his sweatshirt that commanded most of her attention. A multi-hued horizon with mountain peaks in the foreground and the word "Deadwood" printed underneath brought back a flood of memories.

"You still have that?" She blurted it without thinking.

Mark looked down at himself. "Most comfortable shirt I own."

"Imagine that." *How ironic.*

Mark looked surprised. "Do you think I would have thrown it out—"

"—after we broke up? Kind of." She'd donated reminders

of their time together before she'd left for Hendricks. T-shirts, cards, the cheap pink Iowa State Fair cowboy hat he'd won for her in a carnival game. She wasn't about to admit it, though.

The cut on his temple had scabbed over. It didn't look as serious now as when she first saw it. "How is your shoulder?"

He lifted his arm at shoulder level and gritted his teeth. "Pretty sore. It's nothing that ice and ibuprofen can't fix, though."

"Are you sure it's not something more?"

"No," he said with a huff. "But I'll give it another few days. If it's not better by the weekend, I'll see a doc."

Janie wrapped her arms around her. Even with damp hair and the triggering sweatshirt, Mark still made her heart flutter.

His brows furrowed for a split second. "So, what's up?"

She let out a big breath. "I got a call from Rose just now. It sounds like Tom wants to back out of catering Monte's wedding."

Mark winced. "Since his life imploded the other day? I get it."

"But Monte and Camilla's wedding is in three weeks. They'll never find someone else to take his place." She glanced around him to look inside the dim cottage, but Mark eased the door closed behind him, stepping onto the porch.

"True," he said. "Do you have any ideas?"

"Yes."

"And let me guess... It involves me because that's why you're here."

She sighed. "It does. But, Mark?"

"What?"

"Please don't think I'm using you to get what I want. I know you have a lot on your plate right now." She flexed her hands after realizing she'd clenched them into fists. "I feel horrible coming to you with this."

He chuckled. "Because that would never occur to you—to use me, right?"

"C'mon. It's Monte and Camilla. I wouldn't ask for just anyone." He might be teasing, but Janie couldn't help feeling she was taking advantage of him.

Mark nodded. "I know. I'd hate to put them through this if there's something we can do."

"Can you talk to Tom, then?"

He grimaced. "The last time I talked to Tom, I was angry because of the crack running across the length of my apartment, something I'd been bugging him about for a month."

She felt the color leave her face. "Oh. Maybe if he'd have been proactive ..."

He let out a deep sigh and looked across the lawn toward the main house. A broad smile took over his face.

"Then I wouldn't be a guest at the Wendell House Resort," Mark said when he looked back at her.

"Just so you know, Mom never makes big breakfasts like that except for the holidays."

He was still smiling. "I remember."

Janie felt a tickle at the back of her throat. Every conversation with him stirred memories. It was frustrating finding such comfort in Mark's presence even as she worked so hard to avoid thinking about him.

"As far as I know, Monte doesn't have any idea there's trouble brewing."

Mark took a step back toward the door and reached blindly for the knob.

"Then I'll keep it on the lowdown. I'll give Tom a call right away."

Janie wanted to hug him. Reliable, trustworthy Mark. He had a way of setting the world right with only a few sentences.

She'd reached her lifetime quota of affectionate displays the other day, though. Her cheeks still burned remembering the way she threw herself into his arms, hugging and kissing him after finding him safe. Surely embarrassed by her behavior, he'd kept it to himself. That's the kind of guy Mark was. She'd made a fool of herself repeatedly throughout their relationship—on purpose and accidentally. He knew when to laugh at her antics and when to keep quiet. Would she ever find someone so attuned to her idiosyncrasies?

The click of the lock brought her back to the present. By the time she found her voice, Mark was already inside again.

"I'll be waiting to hear from you," she said to the closed blue door.

Chapter Fourteen

Phone calls to his insurance company and sleepless nights comprised the last few days. Top off the chaos with internet searches for a new place to live and short, frustrating spurts of writing on his phone, and Mark was almost ready to buy another pickup camper and live in a park somewhere. If only he hadn't sold that camper when he moved back to town.

He'd called Tom as soon as Janie returned to the house that morning, thankful to have a task outside of work and cobbling his living situation back together. Staying in Janie's cottage while she holed up in the main house weighed heavily on his conscience. Truthfully, he'd almost suggested they swap. Janie was everywhere around this quaint space. The lavender-and-eucalyptus lotion she still used sat on her dresser. A photo of her and her sisters in the white-and-gold frame that he'd taken on a family trip to Galveston. Shirts he recognized still hung in her closet. But then he decided against it. Asking for a switch would only cue her in to his feelings. The last thing he wanted was to dredge up the past for both their sakes.

Tom agreed to see him in between meetings with his insurance agent and attorney after lunch. He'd put in another solid hour of writing the profile for a newly opened restaurant in Rock Island, then called it quits for the afternoon.

Now he walked around the corner of Main and onto Cotter Avenue. Up ahead, the red mug cut-out sign for Daily Grind Coffee swung in the slight breeze. He rounded the little decorative, iron fence that held an unruly grouping of coneflowers and bee balm at bay and made his way to the front door of the diminutive Victorian house turned coffee shop. He was pretty sure the owner still lived on the second story.

"Hey, Mark."

Tom was seated close to the door near the front bay window. He looked like he'd been through the wringer. Already a wiry sort, the shadows under his sharp cheekbones were deeper. Tom rarely slowed down. Now it looked like he could use a week's worth of sleep.

"You look about how I feel," Tom said. "I hope your insurance company is more responsive than mine."

Mark pulled out a seat opposite Tom. "No complaints, except I could use the money yesterday." He was still a little sore at the man for blowing off his concerns about the ceiling cracks. But considering the situation could have turned out much worse, Mark chose to be thankful for escaping in time. There was no sense in looking back.

"You and me both." He leaned forward and lowered his voice. "Though had we not been flooded first, there would have been a good stash of cash in the safe after the weekend. So, I guess it's a blessing the safe was empty."

"And the restaurant too."

Tom's eyes bugged out, and he swept a hand through his

hair. "Definitely. I can't even think about someone being in there when it went down. The what ifs make me sick to my stomach." He nodded to the small silver pot in the middle of the table and the empty mug beside it. "Coffee?"

"Please. I know it's early, but do you think you'll rebuild?" He dumped a packet of sugar into the cup while Tom poured.

"Ideally, yes. But I'll have to see how it all shakes out with insurance. Having already filed a claim for the flooding, it'll be tricky." Tom poured coffee into his own mug. "How about you? Where are you staying?"

"The Wendells' place."

"Are you and Janie back together?"

"No, we're friends. I'm staying in the guest cottage." He clenched his jaw. The perpetual question.

"Ah, that's too bad. You two were ..."

Tom quit mid-sentence when he looked at Mark. His irritation was apparently written on his face.

"Sorry," Tom said. "Didn't mean to hit a nerve."

"It's all right. I'm looking for something more permanent obviously." He cringed inwardly at his choice of words. Permanent *housing*, not a permanent *relationship*. "I think I'm finished with renting."

"Will you settle in town?"

"If I find the right place."

Tom's expression told Mark the man sympathized. This whole situation affected more than just Tom Hicklebourne.

"My guess is you didn't come by to talk about housing, though," he said.

"Correct. I heard through the grapevine you're thinking about backing out of catering Monte's wedding."

Tom slumped against the back of his seat and rubbed the side of his face.

"I didn't mean for that to make the rounds so quick."

"I wouldn't worry about that." Mark topped off Tom's coffee, then his own. "Rose told Janie, who passed it along to me. Rose isn't one to spread gossip. She only told Janie because she knows her sister will come up with a million and one ways to make it happen."

"So talking to me is the first step," Tom said. He frowned. "I just don't know how I'd feed over one hundred people without a restaurant to cook in and staff to serve. The kitchen at the barn doesn't even have a double oven."

"I know. You're overwhelmed. But if we can come up with a solution, it might save Monte and Camilla the stress."

Tom bowed his head, thinking. "*If* I can find another place to cook. *If* I can find another staff to serve. *If* this can all stay under the radar because my permits are nonexistent at this point."

"I get it. So you'll at least let Janie and me try to come up with something?"

Tom frowned. "Like I said, my mental state is at capacity. I won't be much help in the troubleshooting department."

"You don't have to worry about it. We'll take care of the brainstorming part and keep you in the loop."

Leaving the coffee shop a few minutes later, Mark meant to slip into his car and call Janie. Farther up the sidewalk, though, Adelia and Jumpin' loaded a library cabinet onto the back of a pickup truck. His first thought was to run ahead to help them, but his shoulder stopped him. He'd be of no use to them, and maybe even risk hurting Jumpin' and Adelia since he couldn't carry a sack of groceries without pain radiating throughout his upper body.

Adelia saw him and waved.

"How are you feeling?" she asked when Mark met them next to the truck. It looked like a struggle, but father and daughter managed to get the bulky piece of furniture into the bed. "Dad told me about your close call the other day. What a nightmare that might have been."

"I'm getting along."

"I was going to give you a call," Adelia said before looking at her father. Unspoken words were exchanged between them before Jumpin' nodded and walked into the shop, leaving her and Mark alone.

"Oh?"

"If you're looking for a place to live, a friend of mine is selling her house on the east side of town. It's not listed yet, but if you'd like to see it, let me know."

"Thanks." He guessed Adelia would be touring it with him if he took her up on the offer. The constant hand on his arm made Adelia's intentions clear. "I'm staying with the Wendells for now while I think about next steps."

"I'm sure they love that," she said before a forced laugh.

"They wouldn't have offered if they didn't like me." He shrugged. "They're good people."

Her smile faltered. "Yes, I've been told."

"So I'm hoping to have that storage locker emptied sooner than I thought." He gestured down the block toward the pile of rubble that was once the Yellow Pier. "This whole thing forced my hand."

Adelia perked up. "That reminds me. I found something

that might interest you." She motioned for him to come inside the shop.

Inside, Jumpin' eased himself onto the stool behind the counter. He unwrapped the plastic from a sandwich then cracked open a can of cola. Spread out in front of him on the counter were dozens of silver coins of all sizes.

"Jumpin', where'd you get all that dough?"

"Found it," he said around a mouthful.

"Like in a treasure chest or something?"

His laugh was a low rumble. "Can't say."

Adelia rolled her eyes as they moved past Jumpin' and headed down one of the aisles.

"They're only worth face value. He picked up someone's coin collection last week—someone who didn't know what to collect."

"But you're not dragging me in here to show me coins."

"You're right. I'm not sure when this came into the shop. I only noticed it today, and I thought of you."

She stopped in front of a glass case filled with costume jewelry, watches, and lighters. There was even more—too much for one to take in all at once. Hat pins, service medals, dog tags. Mark didn't know what he was looking at, so he waited for her to point it out.

Adelia walked to the back of the case and slid open the door. Her hand took something from the second shelf from the bottom. Before she let him see it, she rested her arms on the top of the case and looked at him squarely.

"I'm not saying I'm sure it was hers, but isn't the resemblance uncanny?"

At first, Mark didn't know why there'd be a thumbnail portrait of him inside this tiny bronze locket with the filagree frame. The clothes the young boy wore in this photo were all wrong. A starched white collar, dark suit coat. An unsmiling, very serious expression for someone so small. It could be him, but of course it wasn't.

"What am I looking at?"

"I was hoping you could tell me," she said. "I'm sure your stepfather unloaded quite a lot of your mother's smaller possessions after she passed. Who knows where he took them. I find it hard to believe my dad wouldn't have known this was hers. He would have seen it and called out the resemblance right away."

When he didn't say anything, Adelia shifted on her feet and cocked her head.

"You've told me you never knew your father."

"So?" He didn't know what Adelia was getting at. All he wanted to do now was call Janie to report what Tom agreed to.

"Can't you see the resemblance?"

He looked again at the boy's face, growing annoyed. "Maybe a little."

Adelia chuckled. "The word 'doppelgänger' came to mind when I saw this."

"To be honest, making guesses about a decades-old photo of someone I may or may not be related to doesn't really thrill me."

"Maybe not, but at the very least, it makes you wonder what else your stepfather discarded and where."

Mark had let go of the resentment long ago. It was too much weight to bear. Now that Sam Ehler was out of his life, Mark found it easier to think of his stepfather in a more neutral light. Sam proved to be a so-so parent for the short time he was in Mark's life. His mother seemed to love him, at least. But when Muriel died, Sam was too preoccupied by his own grief to have energy left to be there for Mark. Thankfully, that indifference didn't seem to apply to Mark's half-sister. He remembered Sam doting on the child.

He looked closer at the photo with edges yellowed with age. *Was* this his father? His grandfather? An uncle? It was hard to date the photo. Maybe this person wasn't related at all.

"Thanks for thinking of me, Adelia." He dropped it back into her hand. "I've kind of written off being able to solve the puzzle from my father's side." He hoped she got the hint.

Adelia opened his fist up again and dropped the locket onto his palm. "If you want it, take it. No one is going to claim it."

"Thanks." He didn't really want it either, but he tucked it into his pocket since Adelia was there.

Still behind the counter when Mark walked up front, Jumpin' scooped handfuls of coins into one of two cloth bags.

"That's not a method I'd recommend for storing a coin collection." Maybe they were nothing special like Adelia said, but he liked giving Jumpin' a hard time.

"This is how they came into the store, so until I figure out what to do with them, the bags it is," he said.

"I'm tempted to take them off your hands just to show them a little respect."

Jumpin' pushed the two bags across the counter toward him in dramatic fashion.

"Take them. I'm sure you can spend them just fine."

Mark's attention fell on an object behind Jumpin', making him forget the coins. The walking cane he'd spotted two weeks ago stood propped up against the wall, its sleek, crooked shape resembling a petrified snake. Even in the shop's dim light, the etched carvings stood out.

"Can I see that again?" He pointed.

Jumpin spun around on the stool. "This old thing?"

"It's different. I like it."

Jumpin' handed it over, an ever-present twinkle in his rheumy eyes. "I've always thought people don't find treasures. The treasures find them."

Mark turned it over in his hands. The carvings reminded him of a book he had as a kid. Each page showed how to draw a different animal. He'd practiced diligently the fox, the bear, and especially the wolf. Whoever carved the animals on this stick had practiced too. The animals were primitive but charming.

The cane felt weightless in his hands as if it was an extension of his limbs. It felt *right*.

"How much?"

Jumpin' wrinkled his nose. "It's yours. I'm tired of tripping over the thing when it falls over."

"You're always trying to give me things."

"What's your point?" Jumpin' rearranged the coin bags on the counter, not looking him in the eye.

"How do you stay in business if you don't let people pay you?"

Jumpin' snorted. "I do. Just not you."

"How'd I get so lucky?"

"You're good company," Jumpin' said with a growl, but he didn't lose that twinkle.

Adelia had come around the counter to stand beside her father. At Jumpin's response, her expression softened when she looked at Mark and she smiled.

"Pops has always been a good judge of character." A flush settled on her cheeks. "I'll walk you out."

Mark slipped his glasses on before they exited the shop and into the stark daylight on Main Street.

"I'll talk to my friend about her timeline for listing her house. I'm sure she'll let you take a peek before it goes on the market."

"Where is it exactly?"

"At the bend in the road where Hickory Grove Road turns into Thistledown Lane."

Janie's street. He'd be neighbors with the Wendells.

Adelia put her hand on his arm. "It was nice to see you again, Mark."

Before he could step away, Adelia slipped her arm around his back. She gave Mark an affectionate rub. It wasn't quite a hug, but it might as well be. She wasn't trying to hide her feelings anymore.

After they said goodbye, Mark slipped into the driver's seat, resting the walking stick upright in the well of the passenger's side of his truck. The brown leather strap dangled against the polished wood. It was just an old, carved-up hickory branch, but to him it felt like a new friend.

Chapter Fifteen

Janie wiped down the last table, ready to call it quits for the afternoon. In the kitchen, Monte's new dishwasher made more noise than a handful of toddlers wielding pots and pans. She didn't have to look in his direction to know Monte wore a scowl. Few things upset him more than someone disrespecting his kitchen equipment. Janie gave the kid two days before getting a talking to if he kept abusing the cookware.

As she stuffed more napkins into the metal holder, Janie glanced through the front window and paused. She'd already noticed Mark's truck parked across the street earlier, but no Mark. He'd probably wandered inside Jumpin's Shoppe of Curious Goods to see his friend, a place Janie could count her visits to on one hand.

But now Mark was back. And he wasn't alone.

That woman she recognized from the week before whom he'd talked with in almost the exact same spot was there again. The more Janie studied them, the more convinced she became they were close. Casual acquaintances didn't stand a foot apart. And she kept touching Mark too.

The more she wanted to look away and shrug it off, the more obsessed she became watching them. Conveniently, the shakers at every table probably needed refilling. Janie hurried to collect them all in a plastic tub and retrieved the salt and pepper containers from the kitchen. She hurried back to the window table and settled into the booth, determined to work and watch them at the same time.

That woman stood on her toes to give him a hug. Even from across the street there was no mistaking her feelings for Mark. *Her Mark.*

Nononono.

Am I out of my mind? He was nowhere near close to being *her Mark.*

She jumped when Monte popped up alongside her.

"What's going on here?" he asked.

"Monte, not now. I'm filling these, and I need to concentrate." He was always nosing his way into her business when it wasn't warranted. Now that woman's hand lingered on Mark's arm. *Does he like all that touching?*

"You got part of that right, the part when you said you need to concentrate." He jammed his hands on his waist.

Mark tilted his head as he talked to her. She'd read somewhere that was a sign of obvious affection. This was like a bad movie—so bad it was impossible to turn it off.

Still distracted, she didn't take her eyes off them even while she poured salt into the shaker.

"I have no idea what you're talking about, Monte."

"If you'd look at what you're doing instead of what's happening across the street, you *would* have an idea."

Janie looked at her progress.

What a mess.

Monte ducked his head to look under the half-drawn shade and clucked his tongue.

"Not this again. You two are kaput, right?" he asked.

"What does that even mean?"

"Done. Finished. Split. Up. For. Good," he said.

"Yes, of course." She swept the salt and pepper granules into her hand, then dumped them into the tub. "Can't I just look out the window?"

"Not when you're wasting the inventory." Monte lumbered away, scuffing his shoes and mumbling under his breath.

Janie finished cleaning up the spilt salt and pepper, and when she looked out the window again, Mark's truck was pulling away from the curb. Janie caught the last glimpse of the short-haired woman as she walked into Jumpin's shop.

She'd finished filling shakers, wiped down the rest of the tables, and clocked out in the kitchen just as her phone rang. Outside, the late-afternoon sun painted the trees in harsh, electric colors. Across Water Street, the brilliant light touched the river's surface too. It was almost too painful to look at for long. Blinded, she didn't know the caller until she put the phone to her ear.

"Janie, are you off work?"

Mark, of course. She took a deep breath.

"Yes."

"I talked to Tom. He's willing to let us come up with an alternative for Monte's wedding. He might not be much help—he's under a lot of pressure—but he said he'd help if he can." He talked so fast he was almost breathless. He was probably still riding the high from talking with his new friend.

"Okay." The word came out clipped. She couldn't muster up the enthusiasm to match his.

"What's wrong?" he asked.

"Nothing."

He paused.

"Should we talk with your sister again?" he continued, with a more measured tone. "Three brains are better than two."

"I'm perfectly capable of talking to my sister." The image of him and that woman standing so close to one another simmered like a bitter brew.

"So...then I'll just wait to hear from you about next steps." Another pause. "Are you sure there's not something else?"

"I'm sure." But nothing could be further from the truth.

After Mark said goodbye, Janie walked past her car, which she'd parked in its usual spot beside the Daisy Gap Cafe. She crossed Main Street and cut between the Shoppe of Curious Goods and Threads Up!, not giving so much as a side eye to Jumpin' Goodwin's store. After crossing Water Street and the bike path, Janie trudged up the small, grassy levy until the newly built steel dock near Kit's boat beckoned her. She scooped up a handful of rocks before opening the small gate and continuing onto the dock. For some reason, the *clang, clang* of her shoes on the metal platform satisfied her. The grating noise matched her sour mood.

She came to the end and stopped. The Mississippi was still, so still that the reflection of the trees across the river cast their images across the water. This part of the river wasn't as wide as it was farther downstream. A buoy bobbed a hundred yards out. Closer, a heron skimmed the water as it flew past her, plucking a fish near the surface, and landed on a rock outcropping at water's edge to her left to eat his fresh catch.

Winding up, Janie pitched the rock as far into the water as she could throw. She immediately felt the burn in her arm from overextending it. But that didn't stop her. She threw a second, and a third. The fourth rock bounced off the dock behind her and hit the side of Kit's boat when she released it far too soon.

Janie heard a muffled yell. Seconds later, Kit stomped up the steps from below deck and came around to face Janie.

"Only you would be making so much noise. And no one has lousier aim than you."

Kit hopped off her boat and onto the dock, scowling while checking the hull.

"I'm sorry."

"What are you so mad about?"

Kit came to stand in front of her with her arms crossed. Her long hair was twisted into a loose braid, trailing over the front of her shoulder. That, coupled with the missing sleeves on her purple plaid shirt, the denim cutoffs, and bare feet, Kit was the picture of a thirty-something tomboy. To Janie, her younger sister also looked a little like a wild sea sprite.

"I'm not mad." She shook her head for emphasis, maybe as much for her own sake as Kit's.

"Baloney. Whenever you're upset, you throw rocks into the river. You've done this for as long as I can remember."

This surprised Janie, that her self-absorbed sister would make such an astute observation about someone else.

A tremble manifested itself on her lips, catching her by surprise. Kit noticed it and her harsh expression softened.

"I've got sun tea in the refrigerator. Come sit with me," Kit said.

Janie's heart still hammered in her chest from her rock-throwing tantrum, and now with tears threatening to spill over, Kit's offer was welcome. She owed it to herself to not overreact, remembering her resolve to get over Mark once and for all. If there was one person to commiserate with who'd perfected a no-nonsense approach to life, it was Kit.

Kit pointed to one of the lounge chairs. "Sit," she said before disappearing around to the other side of the boat. Seconds later, she carried over a clear jug of rich, dark tea in one hand and two red, plastic cups in the other. Kit sat on an overturned bucket and set to pouring the both of them some tea.

"Talk to me," Kit said after handing Janie a cup.

Janie sighed deeply and rested her head against the chair. "I don't know, Kit. I thought it would be easy, coming back here."

"Seriously? It's home."

"I know. It's just...I can't even put my finger on it." She didn't mean to sound so ambiguous. And she certainly didn't want Kit or the rest of her family thinking she didn't love living in such close proximity to them.

"Being back home isn't really the problem, Janie. Who do you think you're fooling?"

She looked sharply at Kit. "What do you mean?"

"You don't have a problem being back home. You love it here. You always have. But now that *he's* back ..."

Janie stared at Kit. Of course her sister would arrive at the root of the problem well before Janie thought she'd catch on.

"And I'm sure it's only made it harder having him in the cottage while you're stuck in your old bedroom."

Janie bit the inside of her cheek. "You have no idea. It's a nightmare."

Kit nodded with a self-satisfied look. "You can't stay away from the window, can you? Wondering what he's doing in there, when you'll catch sight of him again? And then there's the whole sleeping in your bed thing."

Janie's head fell back against the chair again, and she groaned.

"I get it," Kit said. "The question is, what are you going to do about the situation?"

She bugged her eyes at her sister. "Nothing, that's what."

Kit gaped at her with a puzzled look. "That doesn't make sense. You're a woman of action. I've looked to you for lessons, sis."

"Really?" This was news. The hugely independent and self-made Kit Wendell admitted having a role model, and it was *her*?

"I said so, didn't I?" Kit said bluntly, maybe now regretting she'd shown her soft side. "So, do you still love him?"

Janie looked away. "I don't know."

"Liar. The answer's written all over your face."

"That's not it."

"So, what's keeping you from starting over?" Kit asked, then sipped her tea.

"He's seeing someone else." There. Saying it made it seem more real. It also embarrassed her, like she admitted failure. Like he'd chosen someone more compatible.

"I don't believe that. Who?"

"I don't remember her name. She hangs out at Jumpin's shop. Short hair. Waifish."

"*Waifish.*" Kit's face pinched while she considered this. "Do you mean Jumpin's daughter, Adelia? No," Kit said with an adamant shake of her head. "The woman is way older than Mark."

"She didn't look that old. And maybe he doesn't care about age. It's a common thing, you know."

"All I know is you and Mark belong together. He didn't have to come back to Port Chance, but he's here now. And living in *your* house."

She wasn't buying it. "I've seen them together twice now. Neither time looked like just casual meetings."

"Do you want me to ask around?"

"*No!*" She didn't need for Mark to catch wind of her prying into his love life. How desperate would that look? But she softened. "I'll find out on my own in due time." She wasn't sure she wanted to go through the trouble anyway. Mark had left once. What's to say he wouldn't leave again? The first time had been hard enough. Her heart wouldn't mend itself if it happened a second time.

Kit took another sip then tossed the rest of her tea overboard. She crumpled the cup and shot a basket into another bucket sitting near the railing.

"I need to get back to painting. If you want to hang around and chat, I can do both pretty well at the same time." Kit stood and walked across the deck, back to where she'd come from earlier.

Janie laughed. "Thanks, Kit. I've got to get back, though."

"Back to staring forlornly out your bedroom window?" Kit joked.

"That's pretty pathetic, isn't it?"

Kit paused mid-step and turned back to Janie.

"Not if you love him."

Chapter Sixteen

Mark had known Janie long enough to realize when she said nothing was wrong, she really meant something was but she wasn't ready to talk about it.

When he didn't see her car in the Wendells' driveway, he doubled back through town to look for her. Her little gray compact was parked in back of the cafe.

Though Daisy Gap was now closed, a brick wedged the back door open, which meant Monte was still inside cleaning. Mark found him in the back corner of the kitchen, counting cash at the little metal desk that he called his office.

"You're a robber's dream." He came up behind Monte who jumped at the sound of his voice. "Back door open. Cash lying around like you've opened another branch of Hill Community Bank."

"And you're a pain, sneaking up on me when I'm closed." He dropped the pile of five-dollar bills on the desk and leaned back in the chair. "Thanks a lot. Now I've lost count."

"Sorry. Is Janie still here?"

Monte spun around in his chair. "No, she left right at two."

"Her car's still here."

"I don't know what to tell you," Monte said with an exaggerated shrug. Then he shook his head and sighed loudly. "You two are crazy."

Mark leaned against the refrigerator and crossed his arms. "What's that supposed to mean?"

"That doesn't need to be translated. It means what it means."

"Now you're talking in riddles."

Monte hooked his hands behind his head. "I told you before you two started dating that it was like watching two Chilean flamingos dance around each other in a mating ritual. It's happening again."

"I forgot you're an expert in South American avian species."

Monte waved him away. "You're missing the point."

"No, I'm not. You think we should still be a couple but can't get our act together."

"Yes."

Mark's face heated from Monte's diagnosis of his Janie-less life.

"For your information, I'm working with her on something that benefits you."

"Oh?"

"Has Tom called you?"

Monte's smile disappeared. "No. Why?"

Mark hoped Tom would at least have clued Monte in by now. Maybe Mark's conversation with Tom indirectly gave him permission to drop catering the wedding completely into Mark's and Janie's laps.

"I don't want you to waste a second worrying about it because Janie and I are taking care of it, but Tom bailed on catering."

Monte's expression didn't change. "I kind of expected it."

"What will Camilla do?"

"Melt down during five minutes of histrionics while I sympathize by making her a big pan of shepherd's pie."

"You're such a good husband-to-be."

"Jealous?"

"Only for the free skillets she's entitled to as often as she wants."

Monte chuckled.

"So, back to Janie. I need to find her so we can plan this thing."

"If I see her, I'll tell her you're dying to get together—"

"Monte ..."

"Get together to plan my wedding reception. What'd you think I meant?" He wheeled around in his chair again to continue counting cash, but not before Mark caught the smirk on his face.

* * *

He left Monte's to sit in his car while he returned a message from his boss, Nell. She'd expressed disappointment in the latest piece he'd turned in. It didn't have "the spark" she'd loved in some of his other work, she'd said. They talked for a few minutes on next steps, and she offered him another deadline to turn in revisions.

Nell's criticism barely registered as he circled the downtown area twice, going down Main Street then coming back east on

Water Street, all the while keeping his eyes on the sidewalk and the doorways of the shops Janie might have visited. Under normal circumstances, criticism like that might have crushed him. But not today. More pressing matters were at hand.

Tempting as it was to park and duck into Threads Up! or the coffee shop—two places he had a good chance of finding Janie—Mark decided against it. That would make him a little desperate.

But aren't you a little desperate, cruising Main Street? Calling her back would take a lot less time than trying to track her down to ask what's wrong.

Mark pulled over to the curb after his second lap.

Yes, he was definitely going about this all wrong. When would he get the hint Janie had moved on? And now he'd committed himself to spending even more time with her while they figured out how to cater this wedding reception. What did he know about serving dozens of guests? Nothing. And this would take time away from work he didn't have to spare.

To his right, her car still sat in one of two spots behind the cafe. To his left, the river continued its lazy course south, indifferent to his dilemma.

A flash of purple near the docks caught his eye. He squinted. It was Kit standing on the deck of her boat. Next to her in a lounge chair, an amber-haired head peeked over the back of a chair. It could only be Janie. She looked like she'd kicked back and planned on staying awhile.

Kit wouldn't mind seeing him. He'd always gotten along with Janie's no-nonsense younger sister. But interrupting their together time didn't seem right today. And if Kit witnessed his desperation too, she'd definitely call him out on it.

Mark watched them for another minute. Animated, Janie must be entertaining Kit with a wild story. Her arms flailed and she sat forward in the chair, almost toppling it with more gestures. Kit's peel of laughter cut through the quiet afternoon.

Mark took that as his cue to head home.

Chapter Seventeen

It was a perfect June day when Janie settled into one of the seats at an umbrella-covered table outside The Daily Grind on their patio. Janie heard from Mark the morning after her talk with Kit on the landing. They'd made arrangements to meet at the coffee shop after her shift, so here she was, notepad ready. With a little less than two weeks until Monte and Camilla's wedding, they needed a game plan—fast.

She'd already ordered and took the liberty of grabbing a cold brew with a shot of vanilla for Mark. *Friends do that, treat each other on occasion, right?* She'd make an extra effort to be friendly since Kit was right. She didn't know for certain Mark was seeing Adelia Goodwin. Appearances were not enough to go on. Her default reaction had always been to make accusations of guilt first until innocence was proven later. Definitely not a recipe for friendship, let alone anything more.

Mark was a few minutes early. He had his phone to his ear when he appeared on the sidewalk. He spotted her, waved, and tucked his phone away as he came through the side garden to the patio.

"Good news," he said as he dropped his leather bag on the ground and pulled out the chair opposite Janie. "Tom said three of his waitstaff would be willing to help at the reception. I'm hoping we can round up a few more so we can check off finding servers from the to-do list."

"I'm sure Billie would be willing to serve too. The cafe will be closed Saturday anyway."

Mark nodded. "Maybe we have that part covered, then." He slipped a legal pad from his bag and jotted down a note.

Janie smiled. She'd always loved how Mark became totally invested when he was needed most. His enthusiasm was infectious, especially when a project involved helping someone he knew. He'd count Monte as his best friend, not just in Port Chance but anywhere. One thing she'd learned early on in her and Mark's relationship was that close connections were hard for him. Growing up knowing his father abandoned him, losing his mother as a teen, and being left with an indifferent stepfather...those were realities which had shaped his world view. So whatever connections he made nowadays usually were the lasting type. Usually.

"What's wrong?" Mark asked.

Janie looked up from where she'd been staring a hole into the table top while these thoughts ran through her mind.

"Nothing. Why?"

"You were frowning." The corners of Mark's mouth dipped in a mock impression, making her smile.

"Daydreaming, I suppose."

Mark's expression lightened. "Good. I was worried you were having second thoughts about stepping up for Monte."

"Me? No way. It'll be a breeze."

Mark's gaze aligned with hers. A *ping* resonated in her chest like an electrical current as he looked at her with a mixture of longing and sadness.

"Thanks. It'll mean a lot to them," he said quietly. He'd rested one hand on the table, and now he slowly turned it palm up as if he wanted her hand. Their fingers were inches apart.

Do NOT take his hand, that voice in her head ordered.

If she touched him, there's no telling what would come out of her mouth. She pulled both of her hands away for the time being, opening her planner to look at her own notes. Thankful for the chance to focus on something other than Mark's face, Janie swallowed. Maybe discussing this over the phone would have been less dangerous.

"I've already lined up my family to bring food. I'm sure we can get more people once I put the word out. If we organize this as a potluck-style meal, we won't have to worry about permits." She tapped her pen on one of her many line items. "Rose has already amended the rental contract for the room by deleting the food clause."

"A potluck? That's a lot of food." He might have turned a shade lighter. "As you know, I'm good for a bag of chips and salsa, but that's about it."

She giggled. "I remember. But where else do you propose we get food on such short notice?"

His blank expression told her he hadn't thought it through yet.

"Even if we put an order in at Good's, it'll be way more than what Tom was going to charge, especially this close to the wedding. And who wants to eat fried chicken and powdered mashed potatoes at a wedding reception anyway?"

"Good point."

"Besides, serving one-hundred twenty-five people is no

different than serving the roast hog church fundraiser at the summer festival or a funeral dinner." She could tell by the skeptical look Mark gave her that he'd only believe her when he saw her plan in action.

Mark sat back in his seat at the same time the woman from inside brought out their drinks. Surprised, he tentatively sipped the drink before slowly setting it down again.

Mark waited for the server to leave.

"You remember what I like." he said.

"I'm a waitress, Mark. Remembering people's food and drink preferences is one of my many gifts," she said, keeping it light. Janie didn't like the way Mark was looking at her again. "And you are a little more than just a customer."

"I was your favorite breakfast customer for a long time."

"You were indeed." She smiled behind her cup. "Good tipper too."

His smile faded, and his expression turned pensive.

"Remember when we spent that first year hitting all the diners up and down River Road each Saturday?" he asked, leaning back and folding his arms across his chest.

She laughed. "How can I forget? You must have spent a small fortune on mediocre hamburger platters and breakfast specials."

Another grin spread across Mark's face at the memory. "And you challenged yourself to order the most eclectic things on the menus."

"Much to my detriment most of the time."

He laughed loudly. "Artichoke and cranberry scone, anyone?"

Janie fake gagged. "You had to bring that one up, didn't you? Worst four dollars ever spent."

"The look on your face at the first bite." Mark shuddered.

"First *and* last bite," she reminded him.

"Did we ever figure out what that other flavor was?"

She shook her head. "I was afraid to ask."

His grin faded into a more serious look again. Mark's shoulders rose and fell with a sigh.

"Can I ask you a question for an honest answer?" he said finally.

She let out a little breathy laugh. "I don't know, Mark. It sounds like trouble."

"Never mind, then." He smiled convincingly, but now she was curious.

"I'm a big girl. Go ahead and ask."

Mark stared at her for a few moments, probably mentally weighing if he dared to or not.

He leaned forward, looking down at his folded hands. "Have you seen anyone since we, ah...broke up?"

She didn't know what she thought would come out of Mark's mouth, but that wasn't it. It was a benign question compared to what she expected.

She sloshed the coffee around in her mug, not meeting his gaze.

"Yes. Maybe five or six."

It was stupid to lie, and she didn't know why she felt compelled to exaggerate. There'd only been one guy named Donny whom she'd met in Hendricks. She knew it wasn't going anywhere after the second date, though. Once he confessed to living paycheck to paycheck because of his obsession with restoring a VW Samba bus, Janie knew he didn't have room in his life for her too. Especially after he asked her to foot the bill for their lunch date. She'd decided dating was too much work;

she needed a longer break after Mark. Somehow that break had stretched all the way up to the present.

Mark winced.

"You?" she asked. His discomfort with the answer gave her an inkling of satisfaction.

"A few," he answered.

"That's not it, is it? What you wanted to ask me." She could tell by the way he chewed on his lip. Was this his way of telling her about Adelia Goodwin?

Oh no. I hope not.

Mark shook his head.

Janie studied him over the top of her cup. He was so handsome, even when worry deepened the lines in his face. She hoped her own expression didn't show any sign of what really weighed on her mind.

Mark cleared his throat. "Would you have come with me three years ago if I had proposed first?"

She sputtered coffee back into her mug. Some went the wrong way down her throat. Coughing, Janie's eyes teared up.

"I'm sorry. I didn't mean to catch you off guard." Mark reached for her hand, but she snatched it away.

"Why are you asking me that now? What good does it do?"

His face fell. "If it might have made a difference, I thought—"

Janie stood up, knocking over her chair. It clattered on the bricks. Everyone's attention was on them now.

"Janie, sit down, please. I'm sorry."

Something lodged in her throat. Her body felt like it was on fire. How could he ask her that after all this time?

"No. I can't, Mark." She'd made a spectacle of herself on the patio. It was time for her to leave.

He gathered his leather bag and coffee. "Then I'm not letting you go without making this right," he said quietly.

They weaved around the tables and followed the brick sidewalk to the front gate. Janie's thoughts whirled, trying to sort out whether she'd overreacted at his surprise question or if there was another underlying reason.

Mark stopped in front of her car at the curb. "Janie, I'm sorry. If I'd have known it would upset you like that—"

"I just don't understand why you'd think to ask me after all this time. It doesn't matter."

"You're right." He pressed his lips together, nodding.

"I mean, we talked about you taking that job and what it meant for our relationship. I'm glad you had your once-in-a-lifetime experience. But I wasn't ready to uproot my life, and I told you so." *Especially without a proposal.*

"You did…" he said, not denying the truth.

Why is he being so agreeable? It would be easier to stay mad if he'd defend himself. If she let the anger brew, she wouldn't cry.

Janie turned away to compose herself. Mark couldn't see how this still affected her, how it seemed like she still pined away for him now that he'd come back to Port Chance. It felt like she was reliving the horrible weeks surrounding their breakup all over again.

Mark touched her arm. "Janie."

She turned again, clenching her jaw.

"I guess I'm trying to sort out where we stand in my own ill-conceived, awkward way. I'm sorry if my coming back to Port Chance has…made it hard. That wasn't my intention."

Her anger flared again. She hated feeling vulnerable. "Then why are you here?"

Mark dropped his chin to his chest. After a long span of seconds, he looked up, but not at her. "It feels like home. I haven't had that feeling in a long time. It took going away for me to come to that conclusion." The skin between his brows pinched together.

The sting of tears made her blink. They'd talked for many hours about their ideas of what home and family meant, and Mark's experience was very different from hers. What a horrible person she'd be if she didn't feel anything but happiness for Mark now that he'd made this realization.

"I'm glad you've found that, Mark."

A small smile lit his face. "Thank you."

Janie needed to leave. A bitter taste still sat at the back of her throat. She was about to hop off the curb and make a beeline for her car door, but he stopped her again.

"Janie?"

"Yes?"

"I'm going to find other living arrangements."

Now she felt guilty. "Mark, no."

"Yes, I have to," he insisted.

"I know you've been looking, but it takes a while so take however long you need."

He shook his head. "I'll be leaving soon. As in the next couple days."

A sick feeling coursed through her again. "There's no rush. You know that."

"I think it's best."

Mark didn't wait for a reply. He walked away, disappearing around the corner a few seconds later.

Janie sat in her car, replaying the conversation.

Was he trying to find closure again now that he was back in

town? Maybe painful memories had resurfaced for him too, and he struggled to sort through them just like she was. But by reacting so strongly to Mark when he asked if a ring would have changed things three years ago, she'd proven she had no desire for a redo.

And now she'd essentially given Mark permission to date Adelia Goodwin.

Chapter Eighteen

What he hadn't told Janie earlier outside the coffee shop was that he'd already asked Monte if he could crash on the pull-out couch in his basement until he found more permanent housing. Maybe the home Adelia's friend was putting on the market would work out, maybe it wouldn't. But he wouldn't spend another night in Janie's cottage if his presence caused her that much pain.

There wasn't much to pack; he'd barely had time to buy himself enough clothing to make it through a few days without having to haul his basket to the little laundromat on Crockett Street. Mark tossed the rest of his clothes in a duffel, plucked his new laptop from the kitchen table, and closed the door of the cottage behind him.

He almost bumped into Sonya who stood in front of him with her hand grasping the bell pull next to the door.

"Mark. You're leaving." She looked at the duffel hanging on his shoulder. "I hope not for good."

"Actually, I'm going to be staying at Monte's." He shrugged. "It's easier."

"Easier?" Her eyes narrowed. "What did she do?"

Mark almost laughed, but the situation was far from funny. Of course Sonya knew her own daughter. She'd nudged her way into a few of his and Janie's altercations during their relationship. The first time this happened, it shocked Mark. They were adults. He religiously guarded his privacy. But then he'd slowly discovered the close relationship Sonya and Aaron shared with their daughters. How they didn't back away from tough topics. How their door was always open for late-night talks, a last-minute meal, or an emergency room visit at three in the morning. He'd never experienced that closeness between parents and children before he dated Janie.

"Nothing. I'm just not...able to work here."

The skeptical look didn't leave her face. "Nonsense," she said flatly. Like Janie, Sonya didn't mince words. But unlike Janie, she was much more even-tempered.

"It's true. I can't focus in someone else's space."

"Why's that?"

Sonya wasn't going to back down. He was also sure that whatever he said would be repeated to Janie, possibly with a little embellishment and a pointed finger.

"I'm a writer, Sonya. We're a sensitive lot when it comes to workplace inspiration."

Her eyes turned to slits. She wasn't buying it, but she also didn't push it further.

"Well, we'll miss you."

Janie definitely won't.

"And if you change your mind, of course you'll always have a place here," Sonya added. She deflated a bit. "You know it broke my heart when—"

"I know, Sonya."

She touched his arm. "I'm happy you'll at least be close by this time. I'm sure Janie feels that way too...in her own way."

* * *

After dumping his things in Monte's garage, Mark headed to work for his weekly meeting with Nell. As soon as he walked into her office, Mark knew the article he'd submitted the other day hit the right chord with her. She picked up the hard copy she must have printed and waved it in celebration.

"This is exactly why we hired you for this job, Mark," she said as she set it down and closed her laptop. "I'm so happy you broke through whatever was holding you back."

"I think I just needed a wake-up call." He pulled up a chair in front of her desk. "Thanks for letting me know it fell short the first time."

Nell's expression turned sympathetic. "I'd hoped I wasn't too abrasive. The last thing I want is to be so critical it blocks you."

"On the contrary, I needed a kick. I pulled out that article you mentioned at last month's meeting to read again. I saw right away what you meant about finding that joy."

"I remember reading that for the first time before we called you for the interview. I thought to myself, 'I need to take that road trip.' It was almost like I was in the backseat," Nell said. "And your travel partner sounded like such a hoot."

"That she was."

"Are you two still together?"

Mark wrinkled his nose. "Not anymore."

"I'm sorry."

He hitched his shoulders and looked down at his lap momentarily. "Wasn't meant to be."

Nell winced. After a pause, she brightened. "On a more positive note, I have a proposal for you. I think you'll love it."

"Let's hear it." He could use a new direction after all that was thrown at him these last two months.

"We've partnered before with the staff in Council Bluffs. A few past employees from here have moved there and vice versa. That was my first job out of college, as a matter of fact."

He nodded, waiting for more details.

"They're short a staff writer, suddenly, and have a new guide coming out, similar in tone to the *Backroads and Byways* articles you did. They'd like to subcontract you for the job. I told them I'd ask."

"Do you have more details?"

She rested her elbows on the desk. "A flat fee for ten to twelve articles about places in and around the city. Travel expenses covered, of course."

"Sounds perfect."

Nell gritted her teeth. "There's a downside, though. You'd have to work out of their office."

"For how long?"

"Six months minimum, and possibly up to a year, since they might decide to expand the project," Nell said. "But there's a housing allowance too."

"And that won't jeopardize my position here? I mean, I'll still have it...when I return?"

"I wouldn't have considered it otherwise."

Council Bluffs was over four hours away. Not exactly a cross-country move, but it would be a long weekend of driving if he chose to come back to Port Chance at the end of the week.

"And if I choose not to take it?"

Nell shrugged. "Then I have someone else in mind, so no worries."

What reason would I have to come back here?

Mark laced his fingers together in his lap, considering it. Flattered that Nell already thought he was up for the challenge, he'd be a fool not to take her up on it.

But his thoughts weren't centered on whether he should take the job or not.

No, instead, he couldn't help but think about Janie.

Chapter Nineteen

The final week leading up to the wedding was unusually calm. Janie kept waiting for something else to go wrong. A catastrophic plumbing problem in the reception barn. Monte's garage filled with floral arrangements and bouquets catching fire. Or Sonya's health taking another turn for the worse. On the contrary, no natural disasters or acts of God interfered during the days leading up to Monte and Camilla's nuptials. Even Sonya got the "all clear" from Dr. Farr at her Tuesday appointment before the wedding. Now that Sonya's color had come back and her appetite had as well, Janie breathed easier. Her mother even joked she'd moved up a slot on her belt from eating three full meals again.

The cottage was especially quiet. Janie moved back the day after Mark cleared out his things. But even though he was gone, she *felt* him there. She half expected to turn around while at her kitchen table and see him reclining on her futon, bare feet kicked up and resting on the arm. He hadn't visited the diner either. She had to keep reminding herself that keeping her distance was the only way to survive living in the same town as Mark.

She thought of these things as she walked across the lawn and into the kitchen where she found Sonya at the counter, chopping yellow bell peppers. Next to her, three giant platters of already-prepared veggies peeked through plastic wrap.

Janie came up behind her to plant a kiss on her cheek. It was so good to finally see her without that conspicuous PICC line taped to her skin.

Sonya stopped chopping to give Janie a once-over.

"You look lovely as usual," she said.

"Thank you. You don't think the dress is a little too much?" Janie smoothed the skirt. She'd decided against the petal-pink dress Becky at Threads Up! had raved about—the one she'd predicted would find Janie a date by evening's end. Janie decided to play it safe with this dress. Its sleek, fuchsia halter-style top was complimented with a flouncy, floral skirt.

"On the contrary, it's absolutely perfect for the occasion. Colorful and fun, just like the happy couple."

"They are that, especially Monte. Can you believe I actually caught him whistling the other day during the breakfast rush?"

Sonya laughed. "I thought he was at his crankiest at that time of the morning."

"Not this week. He should get married more often." Janie surveyed the mounds of fresh veggies her mother had already prepped. "Do you need any more help?"

Sonya set the knife in the sink, rinsed her hands, then towel dried them.

"Can you finish up here then transfer these three trays to the car? I need to get dressed."

"Of course."

It didn't take but another five minutes to cut the remaining peppers and arrange them on the tray. She floated two pieces of plastic wrap over them, secured the edges, and was about to take them to the car when Kit's frantic text came through—she'd pulled the tiny zipperhead off of her dress. Now it wouldn't close.

Come over to Mom and Dad's. I'll safety pin it.

On my way, Kit answered.

There was a knock on the back door, making her jump. It couldn't be Kit unless she'd already been in the driveway when she texted.

Janie reached for the door while balancing one platter in her other hand.

When she opened it, the veggies almost met their demise on the floor.

Mark.

Looking like he'd stepped right out of a wedding photo shoot.

Black tux. Burnt-orange bowtie. And a half-smile that put all the cover model smirks to shame. She hadn't seen him since they met at the Daily Grind almost two weeks ago.

"Hello," she managed to squeak. Beside her, Sonya gently took the platter from her, probably sensing an imminent disaster. "I...you...left already. No?"

His smile broadened before he ducked his head, giving her a few extra seconds to let her brain catch up to her mouth.

"It's so nice to see you, Mark," Sonya said.

"Rose mentioned you might need help taking food to the reception"—he held his hands out—"so here I am."

Yes, you are.

She caught maybe half of his words, and cobbled together

the rest of what he said. When Mark Christie shows up wearing a tux, minds go numb. Forget that fresh new rule of keeping her distance from him. No, her high-heeled feet seemed to be cemented to the kitchen floor.

"That's sweet of you, Mark. I'll help you take these trays out." Sonya nudged her with an elbow. "Janie? Can you collect the fruit bowls from the refrigerator in the garage?"

She'd already failed miserably at getting the veggies into the car before her mother reappeared downstairs. Now Sonya trusted her with the fruit? Her mother had more faith than she did at the moment.

Her robotic movements managed to get her from the house to the hulking refrigerator in the garage without tripping or flying headfirst into a wall. Janie pressed her face against the freezer door to cool her flushed skin before she opened the lower door. Jasper, the one-eyed calico Sonya saved from a run-in with the neighbor's overzealous Newfoundland, wound around her legs, mewling.

"You and me both, buddy," she murmured. Through the dirty, streaked window in the garage, Janie saw Mark and Sonya load the food trays into the back of the Suburban. She'd have to thank her mother later. Janie needed a reset after the surprise.

Outside, Janie pep-talked her way to the car. Sonya and Mark continued their conversation as they watched her approach.

"Janie, Mark tells me he toured the Hamptons' house last weekend," Sonya said joyfully. "You didn't tell me."

"I didn't know." *What?! The strong possibility of him staying in Port Chance was one thing. Sharing a property boundary was something else entirely.* She took longer than was necessary to arrange the fruit bowls in the back of the car, hoping the shock didn't show on her face.

Sonya bounced on her heels. "Now you do. We might be neighbors." She gave him a hearty pat on the back.

The three of them heard the sound of car tires kicking up gravel at the same time. Kit's truck barreled toward them down the driveway.

"What's she doing here?" Sonya asked.

"A wardrobe malfunction."

Sonya sighed. "That's my girl."

Janie steeled herself for the possibility that Kit might say something to embarrass her in front of Mark. Kit and Mark shared the same dry sense of humor and a special talent for pushing her buttons for their mutual enjoyment. Janie let them have their fun only because she loved the times when her family seemed liked Mark's family. Now, it'd just be awkward.

"Look who's having a party without me," Kit hollered as she hopped from the truck. "I had to bust my zipper in order to come across this fiesta."

"It wasn't officially classified a party until you showed up," Mark said.

"That's just like Janie to leave me out of the loop. She's always been afraid I'd steal you away." Kit rolled her eyes and shimmied up to Mark with an exaggerated flirty look.

Mark played along by offering a hand. Kit took it, twirled twice, then fell backward against him in a swoon. His timing in catching her was spot on. They laughed gleefully.

"I'm so glad someone has a sense of humor around here," Kit said, then pulled a frown. She looked pointedly at Janie.

"If I only had broken zippers and poking fun at family to worry about, I'd be flying high too," Janie said.

Sonya inspected Kit's zipper, declaring it a bona fide disaster, then headed back to the house to finish getting ready. She wasted no time letting Kit know she didn't have time for it.

Kit turned away from Janie to let her make her own assessment, talking to Janie over her shoulder.

"I called Sadie first, but she didn't answer."

"She never answers your calls." Janie pulled the zipper all the way to the bottom to try rethreading it. "Or anyone's for that matter."

"Right? And Rose has enough wardrobe problems to deal with between Jordan and her kids. You just have yourself. And Mark." She winked in his direction.

Kit didn't pause.

"I heard you're buying the Hamptons' place. Congratulations," said Kit.

"It's not a done deal yet," he said with a quick glance in Janie's direction.

Thankfully, she had the zipper to focus on. She didn't trust herself not to give Kit a death stare. First Mom, now Kit.

"I heard that kitchen needs some work." Kit said.

"It's a good thing I'm not fussy, then," he said.

"Lucky you, we have two people in the family who can handle a saw and nail gun like pros. Isn't that right, Janie?"

"Yup." She eased the zipper up slowly, making sure it caught all the teeth. "Can you stop moving, please?"

Kit straightened, pasting her arms at her sides. "Anyway, let me know if you need help."

"Thanks," he said.

"And I'm sure Janie would be happy to lend a hand too."

"All done." She gave Kit a brusque pat on the back. "That

sucker isn't coming down now. You'll have to rip the dress to take it off tonight."

"But this is my favorite dress. My *only* dress."

"Sorry." Janie backed away.

"Are we riding together?" Kit asked.

"I said so, didn't I?" she answered.

"But where are you going?"

Janie fought the plum-sized lump in her throat as she race-walked toward the house. She couldn't stand another minute of Kit's teasing. Or Mark's loaded looks. Having fun at her expense had reached the limit.

"Need to grab my bag inside, then we should get going. Bye, Mark," she called when she was certain her voice wouldn't wobble or crack.

Kit didn't even try to lower her voice.

"Don't sweat it. She's still in love with you."

Wedding ceremonies always brought tears to Janie's eyes at some point between the groomsmen lining up at the front of the church and the bride walking up the aisle. Today they threatened to spill even before she made it inside the church. Janie felt like a pincushion, sensitive to even the most innocuous detail. Ever since Mark showed up at the back door earlier, taking her by surprise, Janie hadn't been able to regain her cool.

If I can get through the ceremony without blubbering, I'll call it a win.

She'd walked up the church steps with Kit and some of Camilla's family members, careful to set a steady foot each time.

Heels were not a staple in her closet; the darned things caused a twisted ankle more than once in her life.

Janie paused at the top step, waiting for the crowd in front to move forward, when she caught sight of the groomsmen on the side lawn next to the church's annex. They milled around, talking and joking, waiting for the ceremony to begin. Mark was one of them, facing away from her.

"Smile. You look like your dog died," Kit joked with a gentle nudge in Janie's ribs.

"I don't have a dog, Kit." She was still sore at Kit for not taking it easy with the teasing.

"But if you did, your face would look like this." Kit leaned forward to see around Janie to the view on the church lawn. Her lips pursed as she looked at Janie. "I take that back. This is your my-ex-should-never-be-allowed-to-have-more fun-than-me look."

The line moved forward. Janie bumped into the lady in front of her, trying to get into the church and out of Mark's sight if he happened to turn around and see her. She apologized when the woman glanced over her shoulder with a cross look.

"I'm not that vindictive. He can have as much fun as he wants," she whispered.

"As long as you don't see him, right?" Kit asked.

"That'd be ideal."

Inside the foyer, she and Kit signed the guest book, then stood in line to be escorted by one of the ushers to their seats. As if the crowded quarters weren't awkward enough, Janie stiffened when the music floating through the sanctuary's opened doors reached her ears. An usher came forward with a smile and his proffered elbow. While Kit chatted amicably with her usher in front, Janie clenched her jaw, hoping no one noticed her quivering chin.

She slid into the pew next to Kit.

"What's wrong now?" Kit whispered-hissed when she got a look at her. She produced a tissue from her bag, handing it over.

"Bach's Arioso, that's what." A tension headache was blooming between her brows.

Kit shook her head impatiently. "What's that supposed to mean?"

"It's one of the processional songs I picked for my own wedding."

Kit looked at her slack-jawed. "Janie, get a grip. Seriously."

"Don't look at me like that. Mark and I talked about wedding music at one point."

Kit's shoulders dropped. "Listen. I feel for you, but this is Monte and Camilla's wedding, not yours. Maybe it'll help if you keep the focus on them." She nodded toward the usher who walked Kit down the aisle. "And I'm pretty sure I didn't see a ring on his finger. Forget Mark's here. Have a good time."

"I thought I'd be okay, but literally everything is a trigger."

Kit took her hand and gave it a reassuring squeeze.

The music transitioned to something Janie didn't recognize a few minutes later. One by one, the groomsmen appeared from a side door near the front of the church. Mark scanned the guests and gave her an almost imperceptible nod when he found her. Janie swallowed and looked away.

Camilla was a lovely if somewhat nervous bride-to-be. Her skin flushed rose underneath her tawny complexion. And Becky at Thread's Up! had been right. The vintage dress was even more beautiful on Camilla, as if it had been made for her. Janie's vision blurred as soon as Camilla wiped her own eyes.

Janie almost admitted defeat when Monte mouthed "I love you" as soon as they joined hands up front. But then the entire congregation reacted with a collective *aww,* which was followed by laughter, and that put a smile on everyone's face, including hers.

The wedding progressed without any more trigger music or moony looks from Mark. And with Monte and Camilla counting on her to move the flowers from the wedding to the reception, Janie didn't have time to seek him out. Plus, Kit was right. There were plenty of ringless guys worthy of her attention. She'd done an outstanding job of ignoring Mark the first few days she realized he'd come back to Port Chance. There was no reason she couldn't continue it for the foreseeable future.

Chapter Twenty

Tom Hicklebourne had come through after all for the main course, smoking his famous brisket for Monte and Camilla's guests. He stood next to the two large smokers he'd removed from the restaurant's back patio well before its collapse. His son and another young man hustled between him and the open back door of the barn's kitchen, carrying aluminum trays of meat.

Janie stood amidst the bustle of pre-reception preparation, covering the meat trays with foil while Tom's wife Donna and their daughter pulled pans of steaming new potatoes from the commercial oven and promptly carried them out to the buffet table in the reception hall.

Across the large stainless counter from Janie, Rose and Kit stuck serving spoons into at least two dozen bowls, casserole dishes, and pans of food prepared by family and friends of Monte and Camilla. When word got out that Tom wouldn't be able to serve a full-fledged meal for the reception, the Wendells' phone started ringing. It warmed Janie's heart to witness how her community always came together in a pinch.

Rose looked up from a corn casserole she'd uncovered.

"As soon as we get the food out, those cupcakes in the bakery need to be brought over for the dessert table," she said. "I'm not sure why they aren't here already."

"I'm on it. Jordan already gave me the key," Janie said.

Leaving the festive reception hall was a welcome respite after the emotional day so far. Outside, the late-afternoon heat had already surrendered to the cooler nighttime air as the sun dipped lower on the horizon. She crossed the gravel parking lot, careful not to lose her footing on the slight slope in the ridiculously high heels. Once she sat down to eat, she'd be kicking those torture contraptions off.

Janie slipped the key into the door of the orchard shop but found it already open. The store was dark except for lights illuminating the bakery kitchen in the far corner.

A woman worked over the counter, stacking one long, rectangular box on top of another. She didn't hear Janie approach over the music coming from the woman's phone next to her.

"Hello?" Janie called out from the center of the store.

The woman stopped stacking boxes and turned, and Janie immediately recognized Linn Miranelli.

"You're just in time," Linn said. "I could use an extra set of hands here."

"I'm sorry to intrude. I didn't think anyone would be in here."

Janie stopped at the counter and looked down at the most incredible cake she'd ever seen. Four white, frosted tiers decorated with winding ivy and pastel-pink and fuchsia flowers sat on their own round platters, waiting to be assembled. Diminutive birds, butterflies, and honeybees made from marzipan flitted amongst the flora too. She honestly struggled to find the most complimentary words worthy of such an exquisite cake.

"That's too stunning to eat, Linn. Seriously, it should be under a glass dome in a pastry museum."

Linn laughed, a light, airy sound. "That does my heart good. Thank you."

"Rose sent me over to get the cupcakes, so tell me what to do."

Linn nodded. "Just having another human being here right now ..." Her voice faded and she laughed again, but this time Janie recognized a tinge of nervousness.

"Sometimes that's enough, isn't it?"

"You have no idea," Linn said. There was an awkward pause before she continued. "I wasn't sure I'd be able to get through today." She spread her hands on the stainless counter, seeming to steady herself.

"Are you all right?"

Linn let out a breath. "I will be. This is the first wedding I've baked for since...since I came to Port Chance."

"I get it. Sometimes it takes a while to get our sea legs again after we've taken time off. Where was home before here?"

Linn kept her eyes on the cakes in front of her. "Burlington."

Janie sensed she wanted to say more, but something held Linn back. If Janie were at the cafe, this would be the point where'd she'd plop herself down opposite Linn, or whomever, and enter friend mode. She'd been told she was an excellent listener.

"What brought you to Port Chance?"

Linn laughed again. "I kind of closed my eyes and put my finger on a map."

"I love that. It takes moxie to start fresh."

"I was terrified."

"But here you are. And this"—Janie nodded toward the cakes—"means you have something solid in place to succeed. Not everyone starting over can say that."

"Your sister and her family have been wonderful."

"I'm happy to hear they've made you feel welcome. Any time you need anything, let me know if I can help."

"Thank you so much," Linn said. Janie detected a waver in her tone.

"Now let's get these cakes to the reception, or we'll have people pounding on the door for their dessert."

Linn smiled broadly. "Good idea."

As she and Linn made three trips back and forth across the gravel drive with the boxed desserts, Janie reflected on the private moment she'd shared with Linn. She couldn't pinpoint why their conversation shifted her mindset, but a new perspective rearranged itself with regards to her and Mark. Her own words while talking to Linn rang in her head again.

A fresh start.

* * *

"Potluck-style wedding meals might become a thing here," Rose whispered in Janie's ear while the waitstaff finished clearing off tables a couple of hours later. In the corner of the room, the deejay announced the dance floor was open after the mother-son dance ended. "I can't thank you and Mark enough for taking charge of that."

"All it took were phone calls. No trouble at all."

Rose wrinkled her nose. "It wasn't too awkward working with him?"

"On the contrary, it helped put things in perspective." She didn't mention that the realization hit her only two hours ago.

"I'm happy you've worked it out." She nodded toward Mark, who stood over the cake table a short distance away with his back to them. "I'd be lying if I said I didn't hope you two could reconcile."

Janie shrugged with a smile, but there it was again, that niggling little spot of hurt springing to life in the pit of her stomach. She pressed a hand to the spot, willing it to go away.

"I'd better see if they need help in the kitchen," Rose said. "And news flash: Linn Miranelli's cakes are to die for. Grab a cupcake quick before they disappear."

After Rose walked back to the kitchen, Janie stood rooted to the spot, hands balled into fists, debating whether to approach Mark or not. He hung over the cake table still, picking up the name cards on each platter of cupcakes. Janie smiled. His sweet tooth was almost as notorious as hers.

She might tease him about his indecisiveness for choosing a cupcake. She could compliment him on how well the tux fit. Maybe she could ask how his new job was going. If she could carry on a short and simple conversation with him, it might end the day on a good note.

Yep, she could handle it.

Her heart galloped in her chest as she drew closer.

Janie put a hand on his shoulder, startling him a little.

"It's hard to decide on one, isn't it?" She eyed the tiers and platters of cupcakes set amongst faux vines and pink and peach roses. Twinkle lights gave everything an otherworldly glow. Linn Miranelli knew how to design a dessert table too.

Mark's shoulders slumped slightly. "I wasn't counting on taking just one." There was already a cupcake on his plate before he plucked a salted caramel one from a silver platter.

Janie dropped her hand. "Then I won't tell."

He leaned toward her as if he had a secret to spill. "Tell me you didn't come over here just to police the cupcakes."

She crossed her arms but stood her ground even though Mark was way too close. "I didn't. I want to apologize." *I do? For what?*

Now Mark turned to fully face her. "Apologize?"

Janie swallowed. It was almost too much, Mark looking the way he did. Handsome, but not so flawless that he was a caricature of male perfection. The slightly tanned face, the laugh lines fanning out from the corners of his eyes, the confusion wrinkling the space between his brows. He was so close, yet so out of reach.

"For my behavior. I've been standoffish. Kinda rude, actually." *Really, Janie? He came for a cupcake, not your guilty confession.*

He gave her a crooked smile. "*Kinda* rude?"

"Yes. And with all you've been through, with your apartment, losing your things." She made a face. "It's been a roller coaster ..." Her voice stalled. She hadn't meant to say that. Roller coaster of emotions was on the tip of her tongue. But that would open herself up to a whole new set of questions she didn't want to answer.

"What's been a roller coaster?"

"Your situation, of course."

"Oh, yes. It has been that." He frowned and turned back to the cupcakes.

She rolled her eyes for almost sabotaging herself before

looking out over the reception hall. Monte and Camilla were in the middle of the floor, leading the people surrounding them in a line dance.

"Do you want to dance?"

Janie chose that very moment to blurt the last thing she expected to fly out of her mouth as Mark took a bite of the cupcake on his plate. His eyes bugged as frosting clung to his lips. He tried to speak, but whatever he said came out as cake-muffled nonsense. If she weren't recovering from her own embarrassment, she would have doubled over laughing.

"Dance?" Mark finally sputtered after licking the frosting away.

Her face flamed at the same time she fought a rising giggle. "Yeah, you know those rhythmic movements people make in time to music?"

Mark heard the laughter in her voice because he couldn't keep the smile off his face either. "And risk stepping on your toes?"

"I'll chance it."

Those devastating wrinkles appeared at the corners of Mark's eyes. Once upon a time she would have pulled him close after he gave her a look like that.

"Don't tell me afterward that you weren't warned," he said.

She could play coy with him all night, but she didn't have time to volley his comment with one of her own because Adelia Goodwin interrupted their conversation at that moment. Janie hadn't even seen her at the ceremony.

"I hope you don't mind if I steal him away. I absolutely love this song," she said with a tight smile.

Janie's heart dropped to her shoes. "Be my guest."

To anyone else, Adelia would have appeared perfectly at

ease. Friendly even. But Janie witnessed enough jealous girl-friends and boyfriends over the years as a waitress to be some-what of an expert at interpreting body language. Adelia's grip was so tight on Mark's arm that the whites of her knuckles showed.

Adelia led Mark to the dance floor, leaving Janie burning up inside. She flexed her hands.

What did *her* body language look like at the moment?

Chapter Twenty-One

Even as Mark took Adelia's hand and wrapped his other arm around her waist for the dance, Janie was the only person on his mind. He watched her as she wandered away from the cake table, hands balled. Only when she sat at one of the tables with her parents and her sister Sadie did she look over at him again. There was no mistaking the fierceness behind her expression.

He'd only seen that look once before: during the fight which set the tone for their breakup.

"Mark, you're a million miles away," said Adelia, who smiled sweetly at him.

He gave himself a mental shake. "I'm sorry. Long day."

"Listen. I hoped to grab you and tell you the good news."

Had Adelia somehow discovered his offer on the house had been accepted before he did? It wouldn't surprise him. People with small-town connections had ways of getting access to private information long before others; he'd found that out during his short time in Port Chance.

"I've found the person who brought in that locket. It was your father's aunt."

This wasn't the news he expected.

"I don't think so. Sam Ehler didn't have an aunt. His parents were both only children."

"No, your *real* father, Dan Christie."

Mark stared at her.

"It's true. His aunt was downsizing and moving across the country. She said the boy in the locket is your father's father."

Wait, what?

Adelia must have read the incredulous look on his face because she went on excitedly.

"You're probably wondering how I made this connection. It was simple really. I looked up your father's name since I subscribe to an ancestry site."

"You looked up my family?"

Adelia nodded. "There are only a handful of Christies in eastern Iowa. I found a woman with Christie as a maiden name who mentioned having Daniel as a family member. Good ol' social media, right? I let the White Pages do the rest of the work."

"But I didn't ask you to go through the trouble." The word "presumptuous" came to mind. "Intrusive" did too.

"I know. But give me a trail to follow and it's hard to keep me away from it. I must have been a bloodhound in a past life." She laughed, then gave him a sympathetic smile. "I'd want to know if I were you."

"Adelia, with all due respect, I don't want to know more. I've never been more than mildly curious about that side of my family." He'd been so uninterested about the locket that he couldn't even remember now where he'd stashed it.

"Really? I'm curious, and we're not even related. Patricia really would like to meet you. She's such a dear."

Mark stopped in the middle of the dance floor. He couldn't believe Adelia had taken it upon herself to track down the former owner of the locket, meet with her, and have a lengthy talk with this stranger about him and his family whom he'd never had contact with in the first place. It felt like an invasion of privacy at the highest level.

"What's wrong?" she asked.

Does she really have no idea?

"I came to the wedding of one of my best friends tonight, not expecting to talk about my estranged family." He wasn't usually so candid, but Adelia's intrusiveness bothered him.

Adelia tried to take his hand, but he didn't want to be touched. "That's fine. I can fill you in tomorrow or the next day."

"I don't think so."

"But don't you see? They don't need to be estranged any more. Patricia wants to reach out."

"No." It was one word, but it did the trick. The smile dropped from Adelia's face like it was weighted with bricks.

"I'm sorry, Mark. I didn't mean to upset you." She reached out to hug him but dropped her arms when he took a step back. The look on her face morphed from mild disappointment into full-fledged regret. "Please, let's not let this get in the way of our friendship."

He softened a bit. If there was anything he liked less than people invading his privacy, it was burning bridges. Mistakes were as human as breathing.

"It won't. If you'll excuse me, though, I'm going to step out for some air." He hoped she'd get the hint and let him escape in peace.

"I'll join you. They have a lovely patio out back that we wanted to check out."

"We?"

She waved at someone across the room. Mark scanned the guests, looking for the person who'd grabbed her attention. Seconds later, a tall, dark-haired man made his way through the crowd, grinning. Adelia reached for his hand and pulled him close.

"Zane, I'd like you to meet Mark." She looked up at this guy like they were more than casual acquaintances. "Mark is an old friend. I've been lucky enough to store some precious family heirlooms for him."

A tattooed arm peeked from underneath the rolled cuffs of Zane's shirt. His grip was solid when he shook Mark's hand. When Adelia suggested they continue the conversation outside, the three of them drifted toward the doors to the patio. So much for escaping.

As he made his way across the room, Mark chanced another look at Janie and immediately regretted it. Instead of burning a hole through his face with her laser focus this time, she'd found one of the ushers, who'd wrapped his arm around the back of her chair. He leaned in to say something in her ear and she threw her head back, laughing.

He loved seeing Janie smile. But she wasn't smiling at him, that's for sure.

And he could take the blame for that.

Chapter Twenty-Two

"Janie, can we talk for a minute?"

She'd seen Mark with Adelia a few minutes ago, and now he was back.

What had they been up to outside during that little private moment together on the back patio, with the romantic string lights and view of the full moon across the orchard? Janie seethed at the thought.

Ty, the ringless usher Kit pointed out at the wedding ceremony, slipped his arm farther around the back of her chair as he looked up at Mark.

"Sure, Mark. What's up?"

"In private," he said, not taking his eyes off of Ty.

She swallowed and nodded toward the exit. "Let's go outside. I can't hear in here." As if on cue, the music swelled even more. The rise and fall of Mark's chest told Janie he was nervous.

That's two of us.

Of course all the different reasons he'd need to talk ASAP swirled around in her overactive imagination. Bad reasons. Life-changing reasons. That he wanted to propose to Adelia and would like her blessing topped them all.

The skin on her elbow almost burned with his touch as he ushered her toward the back exit. When his hand slipped to her back a moment later as they passed the restrooms, Janie separated herself with a quick step forward. Her concentration was already shot.

Outside, dusk had settled across the landscape. What little light was left from the day lit his eyes like the blue-green water of the western inlet in Upton. She could stand in this spot forever and never grow weary of staring at him.

"Sorry for tearing you away from the fun," he started with an expectant look.

If he was fishing for the scoop on Ty, he'd have to wait a long time. Ty already proved himself to be funny but completely self-centered. Janie wrote him off before she even learned his last name.

"What is it, Mark?"

Mark reached for her hand. Shocked, she let him take it, steeling herself for what was to come.

"You know Adelia, right? John Goodwin's daughter." He paused and looked at the ground. "Maybe you don't care to hear this, but I'm going to tell you anyway. It's important to me."

Here it is.

He'd choked on the last few words. The garbled syllables stuck in his throat, and they bobbed underneath the rippling skin, skin she'd breathed in on so many occasions until she was dizzy with desire. She was so familiar with his scent, she could conjure it up if she sat still and closed her eyes. His favorite cologne had become her favorite too. Citrus and oak. She could picture the cobalt glass bottle sitting on his armoire, the sun cutting through it, casting a blue spot on the cream-colored walls of his old apartment.

She let go of his hand.

"You...you've—" she said, struggling to finish the sentence. "I really can't do this anymore, Mark. Why can't we...not do this?"

"Do what? Hear me out. Like it or not, you're important to me, and you deserve to know."

"I don't want to know anything." If he thought she'd be honored to grant him and Adelia a blessing, he was crazy.

"But it might help us both move forward, figure out where we stand with—"

"*No!*"

For an unguarded moment or two, Janie thought maybe the magic of the night, of seeing his best friend marry, would change something between them. That she and Mark might see a way forward together after all. It would take work, and a hard reset as Linn unknowingly reminded her, but it *was* possible.

She'd always loved how he inclined his head when he looked at her and his brows bunched together the slightest bit. Mark looked at her this way now. There was always that little smile too, signs that he loved her. It had been so plain to see before they broke it off.

But now? Janie knew it had been her imagination all along because he didn't love her anymore. Body language and facial expressions were hardly a sign of devotion; it was all so superficial. If they were, she and Mark would still be together. He wouldn't be about to spill the details of a proposal to someone else.

Mark's pained expression told her all she needed to know.

Janie couldn't stand to hear a word more. Mark reached for her again, but she threw up her hands to ward him off. He couldn't touch her, or even speak to her at this point. She felt so fragile that a word from him might make her heart crumble into sand.

"Janie, wait. It's not what you—"

His words faded as the rushing sound between her ears drowned him out. Janie walked away, feeling the stiffness of her movements and the tension holding her shoulders aloft. A gnawing pain bloomed in her chest, growing more acute with each step. It took every fiber of her being not to stop, turn around, and run back to him.

To feel his arms around her one last time. But no. It was too late.

She couldn't go there again. Not now. Not ever.

She rounded the corner of the building as the first sob escaped. Now that she was out of sight and away from his gaze which had surely bored into her back, she doubled over as she leaned against the side of the barn. Janie pressed her forearm against her mouth as she fought to control the sobs. Her chest heaved as she stared through her tears.

No, she absolutely would not cry another tear because of Mark Christie. It was over before they even returned to Port Chance this second time. The silly thoughts of reuniting got the better of her once she found him here again. She'd always been a sucker for romantic reunions.

But there would be no romantic reunion for her and Mark.

Happily-ever-afters were for fairytales and people like her parents. Rose and Jordan too.

She swiped an arm angrily across her face to dry the tears as she marched across the farm and through the parking lot. As soon as she started down the gravel drive, not knowing where she was headed—only that she had to put as much distance between her and Mark as possible now—did she slow down.

It was getting dark. Her car keys were in her bag, which was looped over the back of the seat she'd been occupying next to Ty. And she still wore these stupid shoes. How had she not broken her neck a hundred times between here and the barn already?

Janie stopped. She looked back at the barn, lit up like one of those little buildings her mother displayed on the fireplace mantel between Thanksgiving and Christmas.

A joyful celebration was taking place inside. Two lives becoming one.

The only thing Janie celebrated at that moment was unbuckling the strap cutting into the top of her foot. She undid the other shoe and pitched them both into the orchard at her right.

She may have lost the love of her life once and for all, but at least her feet didn't hurt anymore.

She crossed the gravel drive to walk on the grassy strip on the other side. There was a little wooden shed at the end of the driveway near the road where her nephews sold vegetables to passersby in the summer. She'd call Kit and wait for her sister to bring her bag. Then she'd go home.

Only her phone was in her bag too.

Tires crunched behind her on the drive.

"Janie!"

She didn't want to face him. The emotional toll of this day had finally caught up to her. There was no telling what might come out of her mouth if he pushed her buttons again. Or maybe she didn't have anything left in her but a mumble or two. Unintelligible sounds. Like a broken washing machine or an electric toothbrush.

"Janie, would you stop, please?"

Mark leaned out his truck window as he slowly rolled up beside her. He put on the brakes.

"Please get in. I wasn't finished."

"There's nothing more to say, Mark." She was so focused on not running into the little shed ahead of her that she wasn't watching where she stepped.

Her foot found a slight dip in the ground.

Janie wobbled, her arms pinwheeling.

White-hot panic flushed across her face. She yelped and toppled to the ground.

Mark stopped the truck and shut it off. He hopped out and dashed over to her.

"Are you all right?"

Even while pain pulsed up her calf, his hands on her skin sent ripples through her body. The top of his head brushed her cheek while he looked at her ankle in the beam of his headlights. Janie inhaled the heady scent of his shampoo. As much as she wanted to ignore her feelings, pretending they didn't exist, deep down, she knew this would never be possible. She'd only be free of Mark Christie when she took her last breath. The realization brought a fresh round of sorrow, knowing he now belonged to someone else.

"Let's get you into the truck."

"I'm fine. I just need to get my keys."

Even in the dark, she felt him frown.

"So, you were heading away from the reception to find them?"

"No. I was going to call Kit."

His silence told her he still wasn't buying her story.

Mark put one arm around her shoulders and one under her arm, lifting her to her feet. They hobbled over to the truck where he hoisted her onto the seat, shut the door, then came around the front of the truck and hopped inside. Mark looked at her, his forehead wrinkling with worry.

"Do you need to go to the ER?" he asked.

"I'm fine. Just take me back."

Mark turned on the truck again and slowly backed up the drive. "Tell me where you left your bag and I'll get it. Then I'm taking you home."

But she suddenly forgot about her bag and car keys and cell phone. The pain in her ankle disappeared too. Janie stared at the object resting against her leg. The flashback of a pleasant memory jarred her, of her and her grandfather, each with a whittling knife in hand, picking, scratching, carving. She hadn't seen it since she was a teenager, long after her grandfather passed away. But now here it was.

So, why was it in Mark's truck?

"What are you doing with Papa's walking stick?"

Chapter Twenty-Three

They drove back to Janie's cottage with the truck windows wide open, the cool air rushing into the cab, pulling at the pins in Janie's hair. Mark had turned off the radio as soon as she asked about the walking stick.

"I just felt a connection to it. Like it was calling my name." It was the third time he tried to explain how he ended up with a walking stick her grandfather had made almost thirty years ago.

"But why that particular object? You're not a hiker."

He lifted his shoulder. "Maybe I'll start."

Janie crossed her arms like she refused to believe he didn't have an ulterior motive.

"I don't understand. You had to somehow know it belonged to our family at some point."

He shook his head. "Not an inkling."

Was her obsession for understanding this Janie's way of avoiding discussing something else? Whatever it was, he'd find a way to tell her what he meant to earlier outside the reception hall.

They drove in silence for the rest of the way. Once the porch lights came into view through the trees, Mark slowed to turn into the Wendells' drive. He passed the garage to continue onto the grassy route a short distance to the cottage. When he parked and came around to Janie's side to help ease her onto the ground from the truck's high seat, her hip slid down the length of his torso, sending shockwaves through him.

"Thank you," Janie said, looking up at him in the darkness, only the whites of her eyes visible. Thankfully, she couldn't see the tense set of his jaw.

"You're welcome," he whispered, because he didn't trust his voice at the moment. He reached into the truck and handed her the walking stick.

She must have noticed his tone changed, though, because she froze. Her mouth parted as if she had something else to say.

All he could focus on was the shine of moisture on her bottom lip and how a strand of hair had caught in her mouth until she tucked it behind her ear.

Janie caught him staring. She seemed to lean forward, but maybe it was an illusion. The thought of tasting those lips again made him almost dizzy.

An owl hooted somewhere high above their heads in the white pines.

Spell broken.

"We should get you inside to check if it's swelling."

Janie nodded. The skin on her throat rippled as she swallowed. "Good idea."

A flurry of moths flitted around the doorway as he helped her over the threshold and settled her onto the couch with the help of the cane. He stuffed two pillows behind her back.

"I remember Papa sitting on the front porch so many

times, whittling those figures," she continued, balancing the cane against the couch so she could prop her leg on a cushion to examine her ankle. There wasn't any bruising—a good sign. "He taught me about wood carving on that stick."

Mark went to her freezer, grabbed a bag of frozen corn, and sat on her coffee table, facing her. When he draped a dish towel over her ankle and set the bag on top of it, she gave him a tentative smile.

"Thank you," she said.

He threaded his fingers together and rested his elbows on his knees.

"You can have it back if you want it. I don't want to keep a family heirloom if it wasn't intended to be given away."

"It had to be my mom," she said as she repositioned the frozen corn. "She isn't very sentimental."

"But you are. You should have it."

"Now I feel bad," she said. "There's a reason you wanted that thing, though I still don't understand it. Such a coincidence, don't you think?"

"Maybe not so much."

She gave him a puzzled look. "What do you mean?"

"I found a relative of my dad. My biological one, Dan Christie."

"Oh, Mark. Really?" She stopped fidgeting with the corn and tucked her hands in her lap. She knew the weight he'd carried not knowing one half of his family and losing his mother so young.

"Actually, it wasn't me who uncovered this. It was Adelia. That's what I was trying to tell you outside the barn."

"I... It was? I thought...never mind. Go on," she said

quietly. A mix of emotions played across Janie's face. Hurt, confusion, a flicker of pleasant surprise.

He told her about the locket in Jumpin's shop, the uncanny resemblance between him and the boy in the photo, and of Adelia's relentless pursuit to find out more. When he told Janie how intrusive Adelia became in tracking down his family, insisting that he meet with a stranger, Janie laughed.

"I'm surprised you're still friends with that woman. No one messes with your privacy," she said.

He stuck his thumb and forefinger an inch apart in front of him. "I came this close to telling her to get lost."

"So, you're not even mildly curious to meet this woman?" she asked.

"That's the thing, Janie. I'm really not. I'm at peace with not knowing these people. I'm just a long-lost relative who they never had the gumption to look up themselves."

"I know you've struggled with it before," she said. "But I'm glad Adelia's presumptuousness reaffirmed your decision to let it go."

"Right. It's better to look toward the future than in the past."

Janie shifted on the couch. "Yeah? Maybe that's why you found the stick."

He studied her face to see if she was humoring him. If Janie was serious, she'd read his mind.

"Jumpin' always claims that people don't find objects, objects find them. Maybe that stick was meant for me because you and I—"

Janie's smile wavered. She was already shaking her head before he finished.

"We've already been through this, Mark. A million times."

She wouldn't even listen to him. Her mind was made up like it had been from the second she laid eyes on him in the cafe about two months ago. He'd tried and failed over and over again.

He stood up from his seat on the coffee table. His face flushed at her unwillingness to even listen.

"Then maybe you're in luck. I'm thinking of taking a job in Council Bluffs."

Janie threw up a hand as if to say "here we go again."

"I'll be out of your face, so there won't be a million and one times."

She nodded toward the door. "Good luck, then."

Mark hoped as he got up and moved toward the door that she'd stop him. Call him to come back and sit down. They'd talk. In the back of his mind, he knew this wouldn't happen. He'd been hopeful ever since he came back to Port Chance, but wishing wouldn't make it so.

As expected, his hopes were met with a very loud silence as he closed the door behind him.

Chapter Twenty-Four

The day after the wedding, Mark took Monte's bike on the river bike path, riding it all the way into Davenport, a thirty-mile round trip. He hadn't been on a bike in ten years at least, but Monte and Camilla had escaped for a long weekend in Duluth, and Mark was alone in Monte's basement, stewing about the night before. He needed to blow off some steam. The trip gave him plenty of time to think.

He'd handled the conversation with Janie on her couch all wrong, but he didn't know how to fix it. Even though the connection between the locket and her grandfather's walking stick made sense to him, he'd come on too strong. He knew Janie was his future, but he wasn't hers now. How would he change her mind?

Mark thought about this for two days until, finally, he'd had enough of staring at his laptop without any work to show for it. He headed into town Tuesday morning for a stop at Jumpin's first. If his confidence didn't lag, he'd visit the diner for lunch too.

Jumpin' was nodding his bald head even before Mark

hopped the curb and ducked under the shop's awning to avoid the steady drizzle. By the look on his face, Jumpin' knew exactly why Mark was paying a visit.

"Hey there, Mark. I suppose you have some questions for me." Jumpin' leaned forward on the rickety bench, which squealed under his weight.

"Oh, a few. Adelia must have given you a heads up?"

He let out a wheezy laugh. "You could say that."

Jumpin' reached into the cooler at his feet and pulled out a cola, handing it to Mark. "Then I'll get right to the point. What can you tell me about that locket Adelia keeps hammering me about?" He popped the can's top and eyed Jumpin' before he took a drink.

Jumpin' shrugged. "It came into the shop years ago. Adelia only found it when she went into one of the cabinets for something else. She saw the resemblance right away."

"Don't you think it's a little coincidental that it turns up in the same small town that I happen to live in? That you live in?"

Jumpin' took a noisy sip of cola. "I don't know what to tell you."

"How about tell me this: what was your connection to my family?"

Jumpin' shrugged. "I knew your mother."

"How come you never mentioned her before? How *well* did you know her?"

Jumpin' shot him a stern look. "Now, if you're thinking what I think you're thinking, that's not the case. We went on a couple dates when you were a little bit, but it ended before it got started."

"Why didn't you ever tell me this?"

"I figured it was water under the bridge. Nothing came of it.

Didn't know if dredging up that part of your life was painful or not."

Mark leaned against the pole next to him. He believed Jumpin'. He'd felt a connection to the old man the first day he walked into the shop, and Mark knew Jumpin' would count him as a friend too.

"That still doesn't tell me how a locket with a photo of someone related to my biological father ended up here." Curiosity had gotten the best of him after all.

Jumpin' sighed, then drained the rest of his cola. He tossed the empty can into the bucket of other discarded soda cans with a clatter.

"She'd met your stepfather and things were getting serious is my guess. One day she showed up with a few boxes of stuff. Knickknacks mostly. Some costume jewelry. A few pieces of depression glass. Nothing special. But that locket was tucked inside a box of photos. I mentioned it, but she didn't take it back."

Mark nodded, waiting to hear more.

"I forgot about the trinket until Adelia found it again," Jumpin' added when Mark didn't say anything.

"So my mother knew Adelia was your daughter when we used to visit her shop." He could've known Jumpin' fifteen years earlier had his mother brought him to Port Chance.

"Do you feel like you're missing something, Mark? That you need answers?"

"No. That's what I told Adelia."

"She can be a bit of a bulldog." Jumpin' chuckled softly. "It sounds like you got your closure long before my daughter thrust that locket into your life. That's probably because you have all you need right here, right now."

Mark nodded. "I suppose you're right." *But the one I need doesn't need me.*

"Some things are worth the trouble, and the rest you gotta let go," Jumpin' said.

Trouble seemed to follow him all over Port Chance these last few months, that was for sure.

"Adelia also mentioned you may have had some trouble to sort out after the wedding," Jumpin' said with a loaded look.

"She's right about that, unfortunately." Adelia had seen him come back to the reception for Janie's bag Saturday night. She'd probably read the look on his face, connecting the dots.

Jumpin' squinted toward the diner across the street. Rain was coming down harder now, but the Daisy Gap Cafe looked like a warm refuge.

"Then what are you waiting for?" Jumpin' asked.

Mark pulled his shirt up over his head as he jogged across the street from Jumpin's shop to the cafe. The rain poured down now in sheets. Under the awning, he shook himself off like a drenched dog, but to no avail. He was soaked to the bone.

He'd hoped Janie caught a ride for her shift since her car wasn't parked in its usual spot. But when he walked through the doors, it was clear she'd taken the day off. Billie and a newer waitress he didn't recognize bustled between tables. In the kitchen, Monte's back-up cook Pete manned the grill.

Mark almost backed right out the door again, but he heard someone call his name. It was Kit, waving from the far side of the dining room.

"Join me?" she said in an unusually chipper tone when he

approached her table. Kit's lunch hour was sacred, which he'd learned the hard way years ago. She'd shooed him away the first time he found her sitting alone one day in the diner, saying she liked to eat by herself.

"Why not." Mark slid into the booth, his wet shirt clinging uncomfortably to his back.

Kit held her finger up to signal Billie and ordered him a coffee when Billie came by the table. Today, Kit had scooted all the way to the wall so she could stretch her legs out on the bench. She rested her chin on her palm and fixed her gaze on him.

"It looks like you need a little warm up," Kit said.

"I need more than that," he mumbled. When he looked up at Kit, she wore an amused expression.

"What'll you have?" She pushed a menu toward him. "My treat."

He sighed. "I can't stay long. I've got a deadline coming up fast."

"You have enough time that you came in here looking for lunch, right? Or was it something—*er*, someone—else you came for?"

There was no denying it. She got him.

Billie returned with Mark's coffee, took their orders, and gathered up the menus. Mark watched her tuck them under her arm as she headed toward the kitchen to relay their orders to Pete.

He eyed Kit again and was met with her usual deadpan expression.

"You came in here looking for Janie?" she asked after he didn't answer the first time.

He nodded. It was funny in a pathetic way how it was so

obvious. And Kit, like Janie, shared the same knack for cutting right to the chase—a double whammy.

"Have you two made your peace yet or not?" she asked.

Mark almost asked which time she meant. Ever since he and Janie realized the other was back in town, they'd shared a roller coaster of interactions.

"Not yet. And I feel a little foolish, like she's given me the message over and over again, but it's not registering here." He rapped on his head with his knuckles.

Her brows lifted.

"And now here I am talking to you about it. Like I've regressed to high school, asking someone else to get the read on a girl for me."

"Funny." Kit chuckled under her breath. She shook her head while she toyed with the condiment holder and shrugged. "Although I did ask, so it's not all on you."

He shrugged in return.

"I've always had luck with the direct approach," she said. "I take it you've tried?"

"So many times."

Kit pressed her lips together while she swirled a straw around in her lemonade. She cocked a brow. "As in, 'I'm sorry, Janie. I handled it all wrong three years ago.' That approach?"

They'd obviously talked.

"It's been so long ago." He paused and took a deep breath. "And things were said in the heat of the moment. I'm not sure anymore how we got to this point."

"I'm not one to break confidences, but I'm going to this time," Kit said.

"You mean Janie's?"

She nodded slowly like she was still weighing if she should do this.

Mark waited. He needed answers.

"I'm a big believer in fate. I know that's a little squirrelly coming from a no-nonsense grump like me, but I do. You two came back to Port Chance within weeks of each other. That means something."

It was a little odd, but unlike Kit, he chalked it up to coincidence.

"But Janie's afraid to take the risk with you again," she said with shrug.

"What risk? I'm back. I've tried to talk to her about starting over, moving forward. The future."

"Maybe so, but what's this I hear about you going to Council Bluffs?"

"It's a short-term job. A year, max."

"That wasn't how she told it."

"She didn't give me a chance to explain."

"Don't you see? It's like it's happening all over again. You leaving. Janie being left behind. By taking that cross-country job three years ago without making a commitment to her first, you punted the ball before she knew the game plan."

"A commitment? We were committed. We'd already been together three years."

"Together. But not *together*, together."

"What does that mean?"

Kit waggled her ring finger at him.

Billie brought their food at that point, but all he did was stare at his food while Kit dug in.

They'd talked about marriage, it was true. He'd lost count—maybe five or six times. They wanted a house with a big, wooded yard. It didn't have to be on the river like the Wendells' house, but it would be nice. A dog, maybe some chickens. But then Janie pushed him for a timeline, and he'd freeze. Every time.

"You're saying if I'd have proposed, we'd be living our best life now?"

Kit mumbled an affirmative with a full mouth.

"So, what do I do?"

Kit took a drink, set the glass down, and pointed her fork at him.

"She'd hang me for what I've told you already. That's something you need to figure out."

Chapter Twenty-Five

The sun beat down on Janie's back as she perched on the wood stool in front of a newer bed of perennials Wednesday morning. The bark mulch she'd emptied into the brick-lined area last month wasn't even settled yet, and these obnoxious honeysuckles had already poked through the woody layer. Thankfully, rain the day before had moistened the ground enough she didn't have to dig up the smaller shoots. She yanked three fistfuls in quick succession, tossed them in the bucket at her side, then zeroed in on a bigger shoot.

She tugged. No luck.

Janie twisted it around her hand twice to get a better grip and pulled again.

A stubborn one. Its roots were embedded deep. It might take a shovel rather than the hand spade to dig it up. For now, she'd snip it at its base and come back to it with the shovel later.

Footsteps whispered across the grass behind her. Before she turned, his voice melted the bitterness that had been brewing inside her since Saturday night.

"I lived in a short-term rental when I worked in Tennessee

years ago. Honeysuckle grew rampant around three sides of the house."

She spun around on the stool and dropped the spade in the grass. Of all the people she didn't expect to see that morning, Mark topped the list. He'd said enough in her living room Saturday night. Old wounds had opened up again as he dealt her fresh pain too. Janie had no idea how long it would take to get over Mark once and for all, but she'd recommitted herself to it.

Mark eased himself down onto a sawed-off stump a few feet away. It'd been slowly deteriorating from the elements, which is why she'd meant to start cutting away at it weeks ago But there was always something more pressing vying for her attention. Mark rested his elbows on his knees, folding his hands together, to watch her war against the foliage.

"Anyway, I was between jobs and, of course, didn't have much money," he continued. "The owner knew this, so he cut a deal with me: get rid of the honeysuckle around the neglected beds and he'd knock a hundred bucks off for the month."

She listened quietly, wondering where Mark was headed with this.

"I didn't just clip them. I dug out the roots too. Worked so hard, I still have scars from the two biggest blisters I earned that summer." He spread out his hands, turning them over to look at the skin.

"But no matter how good that landscaping looked when I finished, new shoots had popped up by the end of my stay," he said.

Mark's face looked drawn as if he'd had trouble sleeping. He was usually a meticulous dresser too. Not formal, but neat. Today his shirt was rumpled. Beard stubble covered his jaw and chin. It was a good look on him, but again, not the norm.

Janie picked up the spade and tapped it against the ground to free it of dirt.

She cleared her throat. "Some things are hard to get rid of. No matter what you do, they keep coming back."

He nodded thoughtfully.

"I thought you'd be long gone by now. Isn't your new job in Council Bluffs calling?

Mark shook his head. "No, Janie, it's not."

"What does that mean, that the opportunity will still be there a year from now and you'll accept it then? Or three years from now you'll decide it's right for you and take off?"

"I'm staying right here. Unless you're coming with me," he said softly.

"Not interested. And, if you don't mind, these weeds won't pick themselves." She half turned around to get back to work, but he wasn't budging.

"Did you know honeysuckle symbolizes true love?" Mark asked.

She scoffed. "That's unfortunate, because I'm definitely not loving them right now."

Mark stood.

Good, leave already. He's finally gotten the message. Now she could finish up this bed. A shower was calling her.

Only Mark stepped closer, his shoes appearing in her field of vision as she concentrated on weeding.

What is he doing? She leaned back to add distance to the sudden lack of space between them. Janie leaned back so far, in fact, that she almost tipped over the stool.

But Mark was there, and in one smooth, seamless motion,

he swept her up and onto her feet. His arm encircled her waist, holding her against the full length of his body.

Lightheaded, Janie gasped for air. It wasn't for the lack of oxygen, but surprise at finding herself inches from Mark's face.

"What—?" she started, but her brain couldn't formulate the rest of the question.

Mark put a finger against her lips.

"Listen to me," he said.

"No, Mark, I—"

"Janie," he said quietly, "stop trying to come up with every reason to avoid me."

"I can't."

"I've spent a lot of time thinking since last Saturday, and I came to a few conclusions. The first one is, I owe you an apology."

"What for?"

"For leaving you the first time. It may have seemed like I walked away because I didn't care, but that's what I thought you'd done to me."

"I did care. But then when you decided to go without me, without assuring me...of...of...never mind." She turned her head away so he wouldn't see how hard she was fighting for control.

"A commitment? I know. I was wrong."

"I needed to get away. Fast."

"I get it," he said.

She leaned on him, suddenly exhausted. Denials and contradictions and the walls she'd so carefully constructed over the last few months crumbled further with every second she clung to Mark. She was so weary from fighting what her heart kept pushing her mind to embrace.

His finger lifted her chin so he could look directly into her eyes.

She could have drowned in those eyes. She *was* drowning. *Careful*, she warned herself.

"I'm not going anywhere, Janie."

She shook her head, trying to release herself from his spell. It would break her if he left again.

"Mark, I can't." She dropped her forehead against his shoulder.

His arms tightened. "I'm not leaving you ever again. Not unless you come with me too."

Tears stung her eyes. "But Port Chance is home. I don't want to be anywhere but here."

"I know. It's my home too."

She pulled away to look up at him. "But what about the Council Bluffs job?"

"It's only temporary, for a year tops. And I won't take it unless you want me to. I'll still have my work here."

Moisture pricked at the corners of her eyes as her mind whirled. They'd still be separated. There still wasn't a long-term commitment. She'd be putting herself in the same vulnerable position again. She shook her head as she mentally underlined these on her list of fears.

"I came over to tell you I signed the contract on the Hickory Grove house this morning."

"Seriously?"

"Dead serious."

A smile pulled at the corners of her mouth. "You'll be right down the road?"

Mark nodded. "Neighbors."

Her grin was so wide it made her cheeks ache.

"I love you, Janie. I've never stopped loving you." He released her to cup the sides of her face with both hands. "And I came to a realization yesterday."

"Which was what?" Her voice was barely a whisper. The intensity of this moment had drained the energy from her. Their lips were a hair apart.

He answered with a kiss so sweet and full of fire that the teardrops clinging to the edges of her eyes trailed down her cheeks. His lips were soft yet intoxicatingly forceful. A heady delight coursed through her, from her heels to the top of her head, then reversed course all over again like a pinball. Dreams of this moment didn't match the power of its reality. Kissing Mark put everything in her life instantly in perfect order. There was nothing she couldn't conquer.

"What was your realization?" she asked again, because if she didn't take a breath now, passing out was a very real possibility.

"That I want to spend the rest of my life making you happy," he answered in a throaty voice.

She tightened her arms around his neck, drawing him close again for another kiss. Good on his word, this one was a perfect beginning.

Chapter Twenty-Six

"Thanks for being patient."

Janie gave him a wink while Mark sat on his truck bed two weeks later, waiting for her to finish inspecting the five large, refurbished furniture pieces she'd labored over the last month. He'd helped her move them out of the old garage turned work shed so she could look over them one last time in the light of day. Then they'd load them onto his truck along with the smaller items she'd made out of reclaimed barn wood—plant stands, shelves, and a child's table and chairs set.

So many hours of sanding, staining, buffing, and polishing. But the three side tables and two chests of drawers looked fantastic, even to his inexperienced eye. He'd seen what people were willing to pay for her pieces at the shows Janie sold at on weekends.

Janie straightened and wiped her hands on the rag she'd tucked into her waistband. "Okay, which ones do you want?"

"For what?"

"*For what*? Your house!"

"I'm not going to accept those. You've spent too much time on them. I can find what I need at Goodwill or another second-hand shop."

Janie came toward him and grabbed both of this hands. "Are you kidding me? I'm not going to let you buy hand-me-downs."

"And you forget I have my mother's furniture still in storage."

"Like I said, hand-me-downs."

He chuckled. "I see what's going on. This is your way of refurnishing my house under the guise of generosity."

She rolled her eyes, fighting a laugh. "What can I say? I love decorating." Her hands ran up the length of his arms until she clasped them against the back of his neck.

"And I love you."

Janie answered him with a quick kiss, but it fanned the embers which always smoldered whenever she was around.

"Careful. If we weren't standing in the middle of your parents' driveway, I might—"

She rested her fingers against his mouth. "Pick which ones you want so we can get these loaded. Then there might be time for more of this." She gave him one more kiss, lingering a little longer on his lips. He knew she was smiling even with his eyes closed.

They walked hand in hand over to the first dresser. A harp-mounted mirror topped the four-drawer oak dresser. The top two side-by-side drawers created a serpentine profile. She'd refinished it with a dark honey stain.

"It's amazing," he said as he ran a hand over the smooth finish. Something engraved into the surface caught his eye. "What's this?"

"That's my new signature. You're looking at a piece by Honeysuckle Lane."

Sure enough, she'd carved the unmistakable fluted blossom into the wood then sanded and sealed it with polyurethane. Upon further inspection, Mark found a similar flower on the tops of the other pieces.

"I thought you hated honeysuckles."

Janie squeezed his hand. "They've suddenly taken on new meaning."

Chapter Twenty-Seven

The house on Hickory Grove Lane had felt like home the minute Janie stepped onto the brick stoop and walked through the round-topped red door. Mark had kept his eyes on her the whole time, curious of her reaction as she made her way through the front room with its green mosaic fireplace and hand-hewn oak mantel to the sunshine-yellow kitchen where she fell in love with the picture window overlooking the park-like backyard. Beyond the lawn, a sliver of the river peeked through the trees.

Her favorite part of the house, though, was the master bedroom. It took up almost half of the house with a fireplace of its own. Windows on three walls lent the room the look of living in a treehouse. Janie could sit for hours on the charming, ivy-walled private patio off the bedroom, accessible through a set of French doors.

She sat there now while the sun dappled the patio bricks. Decades of rain, frost, and snow had weathered the bricks, and moss even grew between the cracks, giving the quaint space an untamed allure. Janie hunched over the iron table, working with her carver's knife to etch a new figure into Papa's walking stick. She blew away shavings, set her knife tip into the wood again, and chipped out the finishing touch.

There.

Inside the house, she heard a door close.

And just in time too.

Janie hid the stick behind her chair and waited.

Seconds later, Mark opened the patio door, looking every bit as handsome as he had the morning that he walked into the Daisy Gap Cafe—and into her life—for the first time. Sometimes it was hard to believe that was almost seven years ago.

"Happy birthday. Again." She reached out to take his hand as he sat down next to her. "Did you have a good day?

Mark stretched out his legs. "I did. Nell brought a cake into the office from the new bakery in Greenhaven."

"Jealous. And you didn't bring me a piece?"

Mark leaned in for a kiss. "I have something sweeter for you," he murmured against her lips.

She couldn't imagine a day when Mark's touch wouldn't work its magic in making her skin break out in goosebumps or her pulse rush like a swollen river.

"Dinner will be ready by six. Dad bought steaks and salmon for the grill. That's okay, isn't it? Sorry, I didn't even ask you."

When she mentioned to Sonya that she wasn't sure what to do for Mark's birthday dinner, the words were barely out of her mouth before her mother suggested a dinner party at their house. He didn't like people fussing over him for his birthday, he'd told her years ago. And she told Sonya this, but her mother waved the idea away. *Mark would never turn away a meal with us.* That part was true.

Mark nodded. "Perfect."

"It's not too much?"

Mark caressed her hand. "We can go out for dinner by ourselves any time."

"Or stay home and cook dinner here," she teased, leaning over to kiss him.

"What's that behind your chair?" Mark asked when she pulled away.

"A surprise."

He leaned to the side to get a clear view. "My walking stick is a surprise?"

She sighed and brought it out from behind her back. "You're the worst when it comes to surprises. You're always messing with the timing."

He laughed. "Sorry."

Janie handed over Papa's stick.

Mark turned it over in his hands, examining the length of it and studying the variety of animals, trees, and flowers that had been carved into the surface over the years. His smile broadened when his attention landed on the newest addition: the initials "M.C." and "J.W." carved into a tree trunk punctuated by a tiny heart in between.

"It's finally complete," Mark mused. "And I didn't even know it wasn't until you added this."

"It took me longer to find my original carving set than it did to finish that. I needed the tiniest tool for this that I didn't have in my newer set."

"Thank you. Now it's even more special." He rested it against the table. "Can I give you a present now."

"Why? It's *your* birthday, not mine."

That mischievous twinkle sparked in his eyes. Janie loved

that look. "If I want to give presents on my birthday, that's my prerogative."

"You're right." She sat up straight, folding her hands in her lap.

"You're getting it now, though, in case you don't like it. Giving it to you in front of your family might be embarrassing if it's not what you expected."

That didn't make sense. "I always love your gifts. And thirty seconds ago I wasn't expecting anything."

He lifted his shoulders. "There's always a first time," he teased.

"Where is it?"

"Close your eyes and hold out your hand."

Never had he been so dramatic with his gift-giving. That was her area of expertise. She did as she was told, waiting for him to plop the gift in her palm.

Instead, he slipped it on her finger.

Janie's breath hitched. She opened her eyes.

"Will you marry me?" he asked at the same time her gaze fell to the diamond ring on her finger.

"Mark!"

He chuckled. "Is that a yes?"

"I never...you know...this ring...amazing!"

Merriment lit his face. "Speak so I can understand you."

She looped her arms around his neck even as she kept her eyes on that ring, spreading her fingers wide to catch the sunlight on its many facets. Janie choked up. Such a small symbol of their love, of their lives becoming one life. Together at last.

"I'm getting nervous," Mark said into her hair. "You're not saying yes."

Janie hugged him tighter and pulled away a little to look him in the eyes.

"Yes, Mark," she said. "Always and forever, yes."

Later that night after dinner, Janie sat around the Wendells' long dining room table with Mark, her parents, sisters, and nephews, eating one of Linn's cakes Sonya had ordered for the occasion. Linn had even added an inconspicuous little heart at the bottom on one side to commemorate the other happy occasion besides Mark's birthday. If Mark hadn't pointed it out, Janie never would have seen it, hidden amongst the sprinkles.

"So, everyone here was privy to the proposal except me?" Janie squeezed his hand, which rested on her knee underneath the table. "Unbelievable."

"Of course. Do you really think your entire family would show up just for my birthday dinner?" Mark asked.

A collective groan from everyone at Mark's self-deprecating remark made him chuckle.

"You're now officially part of this family, Mark. You'll never get rid of us," Kit crowed.

"Like it or not," chimed in Rose.

Aaron leaned back in his chair and threaded his fingers together over his stomach. "I hope you know what you're getting yourself into, son," he said with a wink.

Janie smiled at their gentle ribbing while she kept her eye on Mark the whole time. He knew exactly what he was getting into, and he loved it. Her family had become his family.

"Toast! We need a toast!" Sonya raised her water glass.

Everyone followed by hoisting their glasses, bottles, and cans.

"To Mark on his birthday," Sonya said. "For being put on this earth as the perfect match for our Janie."

Mark's eyes grew glassy which in turn made Sonya start to tear up. Then, before too long, Rose swiped the corner of her eye and Sadie ran to the bathroom for a box of tissues. Kit, Jordan, and her father rolled their eyes and fake sobbed so the others didn't think them insensitive. The chain reaction tear fest got them all laughing, of course. It was the happiest ending to the most perfect day.

Janie rested her arm around the back of his chair as she enjoyed Mark pretending he hadn't gotten emotional about Sonya's welcome-to-the-family toast. Everyone at the table had turned their attention to Rose's five-year-old twins who were competing at trying to lick frosting off their noses.

"You don't have to hide it, you know."

Mark indiscreetly rubbed his eye yet again. "Hide what?"

"Your feelings about what Mom said."

He blew air out of his cheeks as if it were nonsense.

"They're pretty great, my family. I'd get emotional too if they totally, one hundred percent embraced me like that—if I weren't already related." He was so fun to tease.

"Oh, yeah?" Mark angled his body toward her. There was a deliciously defiant spark in his eyes. His mouth quirked with a barely concealed grin. "You do know they were pulling for me all along, right?"

Janie drank in the irresistible charm of her husband-to-be, even as Mark playfully pushed her buttons.

"I know they were." She smiled. It was impossible not to with this man. "I was too."

. . .

Are you ready to read Apple Blossom Dreams, Book #2? Download it now.

A Special Note to Readers

Thank you for reading *That Woman on Thistledown Lane*. I hope you enjoyed Janie's and Mark's story as much as I loved writing it. If you haven't read their prequel story yet, *French Toast with a Side of Love*, you can join my newsletter Welcome to the Sweet Life to access it and other free content.

And, of course, if you enjoyed That Woman on Thistledown Lane, I would love for you to leave a review on Amazon and/or Goodreads!

Happy Reading!

Dawn

Acknowledgments

It's hard to believe this first book in the Port Chance series represents the beginning of my third sweet romance series. When I published Bingo Summer in 2014 I never dreamed I'd switch from writing middle grade stories to romance. It's certainly been an exciting and challenging ride.

I'm lucky to have so many people walking beside me as I continue my creative journey. Some have been with me from the beginning, others have just joined. My family continues to be my foundation, supporting me with love and understanding when I need just a little more quiet time to write. To Dave, Hayley, Brandon, Jack, Josh, Em, Eliana, thank you *so so* much.

To my editor Sara West and Mary Ellen Cox for getting this book into shape. You have no idea what a comfort it is to have your expertise and eyes on the manuscript before it becomes a book.

To Wilette Cruz for the loveliest cover. It was such a pleasure working with you.

To Debbie Quain for inspiring Apple Hill Orchard, one of the prominent places readers visited in this book and will continue to see in this series.

To my longtime early readers: Elaine, Nati, Norma Jean, Rochelle, Valri, Maria, Lucia, Bernadette, Vivian, Samantha, Jacqueline, Jan, Erralee, Melissa, Kirby, Katrina, Christie, and Shanna. You are all the best for inspiring me to present you with the best book I can before I release it out into the world. Thank you so much!

Also by D.E. Malone

Hearts in Hendricks series

Love Like Water

Love Like Fire

Love Like Air

Love Like Forever

Blueberry Point Romance series

Love, Lies and Lavender

Love, Lies and Mistletoe

Love, Lies and Lullabies

Love, Lies and Lemon Pie

Love, Lies and Sleigh Rides

Love, Lies and Valentines

Love, Lies and Literature

Blueberry Point Romance Collection (four novellas)

Port Chance series

Apple Blossom Dreams

A Forever Kiss in Silver Leaf Falls

About the Author

D.E. Malone writes contemporary romance and is the author of the Hearts in Hendricks and Blueberry Point romance series. Her work has appeared in the Chicken Soup for the Soul series, *Highlights for Children*, and other publications. When not writing, she loves outdoors—gardening, hiking, and exploring places off-the-beaten path. She lives in central Illinois with her husband.